D1624505

Afterward

ALSO BY CATHERINE M. RAE

Brownstone Facade
Julia's Story
Sarah Cobb

Catherine M. Rae

Afterward

St. Martin's Press   New York

FICTION

AFTERWARD. Copyright © 1992 by Catherine M. Rae. All rights reserved. Printed in the United States of America. No part of this book may be used or reproduced in any manner whatsoever without written permission except in the case of brief quotations embodied in critical articles or reviews. For information, address St. Martin's Press, 175 Fifth Avenue, New York, N.Y. 10010.

Design by Judith A. Stagnitto

Library of Congress Cataloging-in-Publication Data

Rae, Catherine M.
     Afterward / Catherine M. Rae.
       p. cm.
     ISBN 0-312-06894-8
     I. Title.
     PS3568.A355A69   1992
     813'.54—dc20
                                       91-40581
                                             CIP

First Edition: March 1992

10 9 8 7 6 5 4 3 2 1

For Kathleen W. Rae
and
André L. Ricciardi

I am indebted to George Dale for his help in the research for this book.

Author's Preface

On June 15, 1904, the *General Slocum,* an excursion boat owned by the Knickerbocker Steamship Company, left the East River pier at the foot of Third Street in Manhattan with banners flying and bands playing. It carried 1,358 passengers, most of them members of St. Mark's Evangelical Lutheran Church on Sixth Street in the heart of the area known as Little Germany. The occasion, that bright, cloudless June day, was the annual church picnic at Locust Grove on the Long Island Sound.

Pastor Haas had chartered the boat for $350, and the night before the outing, men from the church carried aboard several barrels containing glasses for beer and other beverages, all packed in salt hay. How a fire started in the salt hay after the glasses had been removed is not clear, but start it did, and because the barrels had been left in a storeroom, it remained unnoticed as it spread belowdecks. By the time the boat reached 110th Street, though, it was engulfed in flames, and when the captain, W. H. Van Schlaick, finally brought it to shore at North Brother Island in the Bronx, it was a charred wreck, with 1,024 of its passengers either dead or missing.

The *General Slocum* had been issued a certificate of inspection only five weeks before it set out on its last voyage. In the subsequent investigation, the United States Steamboat Service, which had been responsible for the inspection, was found negligent on several counts. The cloth fire hoses had so deteriorated that when water was pumped into them, they burst open; the canvas life jackets that had hung on their racks for years fell apart, their cork filling nothing but dust; and the life rafts were fastened so firmly to the decks that the frenzied passengers could not pry them loose.

When President Theodore Roosevelt read the report of the federal commission he had appointed to investigate the matter, he issued an order for the immediate removal of the inspectors. They were not prosecuted. Captain Van Schlaick, however, was found guilty of failing to maintain his ship properly, and sentenced to ten years in Sing Sing. He was later pardoned by President Taft.

These are known facts about one of the worst shipping disasters in the United States. What has remained unknown is what happened to the families of the victims—afterward.

I

JANUARY 1919

I have heard it said that there is nothing so powerful as a brush with death to cause a person to reexamine his life, but I never gave the statement more than a passing thought until a few weeks ago when my strength began to return after a long and at times desperate battle with influenza. I've been told that I am one of the fortunate ones, that more than half a million people, the majority in the Northeast, succumbed to the disease last fall. What should have been a time of rejoicing and celebration that the war in Europe was over and that the troops were returning home was a time of mourning and despair for many households.

I was almost in despair myself when I saw my reflection in the cheval glass in my bedroom after the fever had left me and I was allowed out of bed. My cheeks were hollow, my eyes seemed abnormally large, my hair was without luster, and my body looked painfully thin. I have never thought of myself as vain, but my appearance so horrified me that when my doctors suggested I recuperate in a warmer climate than New York has to offer during the winter months, I jumped at the chance, more to avoid curious or pitying glances than anything else.

I am quite comfortable here in central Florida, in what is more like a luxurious hotel than a convalescent home (which it really is). If there are any extremely ill or dying patients, they must be in one of the annexes, for I have neither seen nor heard them. The only people I have seen other than the staff are, like me, here to regain their strength after an illness, and we are treated like honored guests at a resort rather than patients.

The rooms are large, airy, and tastefully furnished; from my windows I have a view of carefully tended gardens beyond which groves of orange trees stretch as far as the eye can see. Every second day I walk over to the clinic, housed in an old-fashioned cottage surrounded by brilliant flowering shrubs, the likes of which I have never seen before. One of the nurses checks my blood pressure and weight, and I am happy to see that I am slowly but steadily gaining back the pounds I lost and beginning to look like my former self.

Strangely enough, time does not hang heavily on my hands, although I am alone most of the time. I do the prescribed walking and resting, and then I read (there is a surprisingly well-stocked library across the hall from the reception room). Almost every evening, however, I retire early to my room. As I sit in front of the wide window open to the warm night air, I let my mind drift back to the past, dwelling as long as I can on the early years, before my life, along with the lives of so many others, was changed by circumstances over which we had no control.

Although the house on Eleventh Street on Manhattan's Lower East Side, in Little Germany, was small for a family of seven and forced us to live more or less on top of one another, no one seemed to mind—but then, we'd never known anything else.

With the exception of Kitty and Megan, who came later, we were all born there: Angie in 1887, myself in 1889, the twins, Robbie and Ralph, in 1892, and Johnnie two years later. I can picture the house now as clearly as if I had walked through it yesterday. Three shallow steps led up to the front door, which opened into a narrow hallway. To the left of the entrance a steep flight of stairs rose to the second floor, while to the right the parlor, with its worn red carpet and faded upholstery, exuded an air of comfort. A short hall led to the kitchen in the rear, where I can almost see Mama turning away from the big black coal stove with a ladle in her hand and hear her say to me: "Maud, set the table, and then call the others; supper is all ready."

Next to the kitchen and partly under the stairs was a small bathroom containing at first only a toilet and washbasin. Later, Papa, who was in the construction business, installed a white porcelain bathtub with claw feet, fitting it neatly into the space under the stairs. Every once in a while there would be a wail of dismay from one of the twins, causing Mama to shake her head and wonder if he'd ever learn that if he didn't crouch when getting into the tub, he'd bump his head on the under-side of one of the stair treads.

On the second floor the bedrooms were small, tiny by today's standards, with barely enough room for the beds and a single dresser. Angie and I had the room in the rear of the house overlooking the backyards with their omnipresent wash-lines. The three boys were in the middle room, and our parents slept in the slightly larger front bedroom whose single window looked out on Eleventh Street.

As I said, we were crowded in those five rooms, and while Mama raised no objection when Angie or I brought a friend home from school in the afternoon, neither did she encourage us to do so. As a result, we often spent a rainy hour or so at Carlotta Schwartz's, Ella Waldman's, or, less frequently, Maria Bishoff's. They all lived in houses identical to ours, but their families were smaller.

Papa was often late coming home in those days. Many a night we would have been fed and our dishes cleared away before he came in. Then, unless he was very late, he and Mama would have their meal together while Angie and I put Johnnie to bed. Then we would do our homework at the table in the parlor, the twins playing some game or other on the floor. It was a comfortable, regulated life, and I remember only one occasion when I was upset—no, I think *frightened* is the better word. On a hot, sultry summer night Angie and I were sitting at the window in our nightgowns waving the little paper fans we had made in an effort to keep cool when the front door slammed so violently that we both jumped.

A moment later we heard Mama's usually gentle voice raised angrily: "John Evans! I'll not stand for it any longer! Have you no feeling for your family at all? Must you go out drinking like a ne'er-do-well every blessed Saturday night? And sometimes weeknights as well?"

"Now, Mary—" Papa sounded contrite.

"Don't you 'now, Mary' me!" she retorted. "You do this once more, and I'll not be here. I'll take the children and go. And you can get your own supper. I want none of your company!"

We dove into bed as she came running up the stairs, and a few moments later we heard the key turn in her bedroom door. I couldn't sleep. I lay in that hot narrow bed staring at the ceiling, wondering what would become of us. Where would we go if Papa came home late again? And where would Mama get any money if she didn't have his wages? Would we have to go to the poorhouse like old Mrs. Weiss after Mr. Weiss fell down the stairs and broke his neck?

I didn't dare go to Mama for comfort, and Angie was no help at all.

"Don't be such a ninny, Maudie. All married people have fights. They'll make it up—you'll see. Go to sleep for heaven's sake," she said crossly.

From then on Papa came home in time for supper.

The boys were probably too young to notice it, but Angie and I were aware of the excitement in the air well before Papa announced that his "ship had come in," that we were no longer poor as churchmice, and that he had rented a house for us in a neighborhood with some "class." We left Eleventh Street and Little Germany forever in the spring of 1897, two days before my eighth birthday.

II

One of my clearest memories of our first year in the four-story house on Thirty-second Street is of coming home with Angie from Miss Lawlor's Private Academy for Girls ("No free public school for my children," Papa boasted) on a blustery winter day and finding Mama next to the fire in the parlor with a tea tray in front of her and a pot of cocoa keeping warm on the hearth for us. It seemed strange at first that she wasn't standing over the range in the kitchen. I think she would have enjoyed doing some of the cooking, but Papa insisted on hiring Mrs. Murphy to cook and Tillie, who looked after Johnnie and later on took charge of Kitty and Megan. And then there was Lizzie, who came in days to do the cleaning and laundry.

"You can't live in a big house like this, Mary," I heard him say shortly after we moved in, "without proper help, and I want you to have it. You've certainly earned a bit of luxury, and now that I can afford to give you some of the good things in life, you'd jolly well better accept them. You know you're all the world to me, don't you, darlin'?"

She was indeed "all the world" to him. He could deny her

nothing (not that she ever asked for much), and I never knew him to be angry with her, as he so often was with us. We were all a bit afraid of his quick temper (Angie not so much as the rest of us) and stayed out of his way when he was worried or upset, especially when Mama was sick, as she was for a long time after Megan's birth. Kitty had been born the year before, and Angie told me she overheard Dr. Sullivan say Mama shouldn't have had another baby so soon.

"Papa didn't like to hear that, Maudie," she said. "but it's about time he learned he can't have his own way in everything. And if he thinks he's going to make me stay in that dreary school much longer, he's in for a surprise."

"What will you do?" I asked, shocked at her audacity.

"You'll see," she replied with a knowing little smile.

Angie had never been a dedicated student, and the only times she was even moderately happy at Miss Lawlor's were when she acted in one of the little plays that were put on two or three times a year. Prettier than anyone else in the school, she was invariably cast as the leading lady, the princess, the queen, or anyone who was supposed to be beautiful. I shall never forget the gasp that went up in the audience when she floated onto the stage as Titania in a scene from *A Midsummer Night's Dream*—"A perfect vision," I heard the portly gentleman sitting behind me say.

She was bright enough and did her work quickly to get it out of the way, but several times during our years at Miss Lawlor's her teachers sent notes home to Papa complaining that she spent too much time gazing out the window and daydreaming instead of concentrating on what the instructor was saying.

"It's all so boring, Papa," she said when he reproved her. "Who cares about the battles in the Civil War, anyway? They're not teaching me anything that will be of any use to me."

Papa sighed, then smiled and patted her shoulder. "Ah, well—books aren't everything, Angie. Your looks will probably get you everything you want in the end."

"Then I needn't go to school any longer?" Angie asked quickly. "I could stay home and help Mama, and go shopping—"

"I didn't say that, my girl. You'll finish out this year—how old are you now, sixteen? And then we'll see."

"You mean until June?" Angie wailed. "It's only December—"

"Enough!" Papa exploded. "You'll do as I say!"

"It's all right for you, Maudie," Angie said when we went up to our room that night. "You *like* school. You read every book you can get your hands on. You don't know what torture it is for me. I can't, and I won't, stand for it much longer."

She did finish out the year, but in the fall of 1903, when the boys and I returned to our respective schools, Angie was permitted to remain at home.

On one of the rare occasions when Mama and I were alone, she told me that Papa was afraid Angie would badger him half to death if he didn't give in. "In any case, Maudie," she continued, "Angie's much happier now. She's like a bird released from its cage, flitting here and there, to her dance lessons or the shops, or visiting the Donellan girls and Geraldine Fawcett. And as you've no doubt noticed, young men are beginning to call on her. It does me good to see her in such high spirits, the way she was as a child in the old house."

I watched her thread a needle, and when I commented on how smooth and white her hands were, she shook her head slightly and smiled over at me. "No matter how poor we were, Maudie, no matter how little money Papa gave me, I always managed to have some kind of old gloves to wear for the heavy work, the scrubbing and all. No, I never worried about my hands. 'Twas my back I feared would give way. Thanks be to God, it's held up—so far.''

Mama seldom spoke of those earlier years, so when she paused and held up the little velvet dress with its Irish-lace collar she was shortening for Megan (I recognized it as one Kitty had outgrown), I thought she'd change the subject. She didn't though. "You and Angie had the worst of it, lovey," she said ruefully. "You never had anything like this to wear when you were little. No Irish lace for you. Coarse gingham was all we could afford on a day laborer's wages."

"But Papa—" I began.

"You wouldn't remember it, Maudie. Until you were four or thereabouts, Papa shoveled and dug and hammered and sawed ten or more hours a day before his chance came. Fortunate for us it was that Matt Bailey knew a good man when he saw one and made him a foreman in the company. And even then it still wasn't easy for a while. Oh, we had more money, but it was scrape and scrimp, buy cheap cuts of meat, and make do, make do, for a couple of years until we had enough money in the bank for Papa to think of starting his own company.''

She paused again and took so long to snip off a few little threads that I thought she'd finished reminiscing.

"That's not what happened, though," she said finally. "Matt Bailey died suddenly, and Papa was able to take over the business, and—" she laughed happily—"we still had money in the bank! And now Papa is the president of the John T. Evans Construction Company! And you know how proud he is at being able to move up in the world. He never liked living in the heart of Little Germany. . . .''

"Why did we live there?" I asked. "We were the only Irish on the block. Angie said once that maybe you wanted us to learn German—"

"Lord bless you, no, lovey!" she said with a laugh. "That

wasn't it at all, although it would do you no harm to know another tongue. No, it was because for the rent we could afford to pay then, it seemed like the best bargain, a nice quiet street—clean, too, with the front steps scrubbed and the garbage pails kept out of sight. It looked like a safe place for children as well. 'Twas I who insisted on taking that house. Your father wasn't too keen on it, ever. And after a while he couldn't wait to get out of it.''

I had any number of questions I wanted to ask her—another opportunity might not come up again soon—but just then the front door slammed, and she started nervously.

"Oh, that'll be Papa now. Don't let on that I've been talking about the old days, lovey. He'd just as soon forget all about them.''

A moment or two later the room seemed to be filled with my father's presence. He wasn't loud or boisterous, but I always felt that he was "in charge" the moment he appeared. He kissed Mama, patted me on the head, and added a few coals to the smoldering fire before he settled down with the evening paper in his big leather chair. I waited a few minutes, then excused myself. I was perceptive enough to know when he wanted Mama to himself.

III

Papa so rarely objected to anything Mama wanted to do that we were all taken by surprise when he made such a fuss about the boat trip on Long Island Sound. As they argued about it at the dinner table that night, I could see that Mama herself was not overly enthusiastic about spending several hours sailing out to Locust Grove for a picnic lunch and several more returning home again. No, she didn't really want to go, but neither did she want to hurt her old friend Mrs. Bosenhart by refusing an invitation extended with genuine warmth and affection.

"I'd much rather stay home, John," she said gently, motioning to Robbie to take his elbows off the table. "But Frieda Bosenhart asked me months ago to save the date. She'd already bought the tickets, and she would have been crushed if I'd refused. It's the annual Lutheran church picnic—you remember St. Mark's—and Pastor Haas has made all the arrangements. Frieda says there'll be a band—"

"And you not even a Lutheran," Papa grumbled. "Oh, you can go, Mary," he went on resignedly. "I never could say no to you, but I don't like it. I don't like it at all." He frowned, and his face began to assume what the twins called his thundery look. "What if a squall comes up? What if the boat springs a leak and—"

"Now, don't be daft, John Evans," Mama interrupted. "I said I'd go, and go I will." She paused for a moment and nodded across the table at me. "And I'll take Maudie with me. She can help keep an eye on Johnnie and the twins. I'd take Angie, too, if she weren't feeling poorly, but as it is, she'll have to stay home with Tillie and the little ones. Just stop your fretting, John. By this time tomorrow, we'll all be sitting right here again with a good meal in front of us."

I glanced over at Angie, who was recovering from what Dr. Sullivan called la grippe, and she smiled wanly at me when I caught her eye. We both thought we knew the real reason Papa objected to the trip: Ever since we'd moved uptown, he'd been anxious to sever all connections with our former humbler environment.

I remember how he'd scowl and change the subject when Angie or I would mention Ella Waldman, Carlotta Schwartz, or some other child we'd known. He'd begin talking about the advantages of living in a good neighborhood, the importance of associating with the "right people," and being seen in the right places.

"Keep away from Third Avenue," he'd say warningly (we lived just east of Fourth Avenue). "No one is to go there, hear? And no one is to ride on the new subway—I don't trust that. When you leave this house, look to the west, toward Madison and Fifth Avenue, where the nobs live. Nothing is to be gained by going east. No sir, the best is in the west, and we're going to have the best there is, that we are." Then he'd beam across the table at Mama.

He'd talk like that when he was feeling mellow, satisfied with himself at the end of dinner after he'd had a few glasses

of wine, completely unaware of the embarrassment his boast-
ing caused us.

The night before the boat trip, however, his mind was not
on his place in society. "I still don't like it," he muttered as
Mama began to serve the pie Mrs. Murphy put in front of her.
"When you get home, Mary, *if* you get home, you'll be all
tired out, and me with two tickets to the opera for tomorrow
night. It's Caruso himself, too, singing *Pagliacci*—"

Fortunately, at that moment Tillie, the nursemaid, came in
with the two little ones, and his attention was diverted. "Ah,
here come my beauties!" he exclaimed, taking Megan on his
lap while Kitty ran to Mama. "Come now, darlin', put your
arm around my neck and let me have a kiss. Ah, that's my
girl."

As he sat smiling down at Megan's curly head while he fed
her bits of piecrust from his plate, I looked around the table,
idly wondering if anyone had already disobeyed him and inves-
tigated the mysteries of Third Avenue and the subway. Angie,
maybe? She was daring enough and had plenty of free time now
that she no longer attended school. Papa called the little ones
his beauties, but I once heard him introduce Angie to a visitor
as "the flower of the family."

At seventeen, she was incredibly lovely. With her deep
blue-violet eyes, softly curling light-brown hair, and a complexion that glowed without the aid of cosmetics, she was
enough to turn any man's head. She'd already had two proposals, one from Lester Elmendorf and the other from Larry
McGuire, both of which Papa rejected on the grounds that she
was too young to consider marriage.

"Age had nothing to do with it, Maudie," she said to me
after Papa had refused Larry's bid for her hand. "He's hoping
I'll meet one of the Astors or Goulds, someone rich, so he can
associate with the 'nobs.' "

"What will you do?" I asked anxiously. I couldn't imagine life without her.

"I'll wait until I'm eighteen, and then I'll marry to suit myself," she said firmly.

Had I been more mature at the time, I would have recognized the force of her determination, but all I could think of then was how lonely I'd be without her. "Aren't you afraid Papa will make an awful fuss?" I asked after a moment or two.

"It won't matter," she answered. "I won't be here. I suppose he'll take it out on the rest of you, but he'll get over it, Maudie, and you must look at it this way: It will make it easier for you to choose your husband when the time comes. Papa will have to realize he can't control everyone's life. Come on, let's walk over to the Ladies' Mile. I need some trimming for a hat."

I was fifteen then and felt awkward and clumsy next to Angie. I was all angles, skinny instead of slender, of medium height, and had a mop of unruly black hair that I hated. My eyes were not the lovely shade of Angie's and although they were blue enough—Mama said they were like an Irish sky—they couldn't compare with hers. And on top of everything else, I had freckles on my nose.

But to get back to the dinner table; Robbie and Ralph, twelve now, were sitting on my side of the table, so I couldn't see their expressions very well, but it wouldn't have surprised me to learn that they'd already made forays into the forbidden territories. They were a good-looking pair who could be a source of delight or exasperation, and the only time they were at all subdued was at meals. Johnnie, at ten, was a serious child, more apt to be found curled up in an easy chair with a book about pirates or jungles than outdoors playing ball with the twins. He and I were the readers.

"You'll ruin your eyes with all that reading," Papa would admonish him. (He never said anything to me when he saw me with a book, leading me to believe he thought reading was not a suitable occupation for boys but quite a proper one for girls.) "Go on, Johnnie, get out in the fresh air. What's the point in having a big backyard if you don't use it?" And Johnnie would pretend to go out, but I knew he'd make straight for the cook's rocking chair in the kitchen.

Angie said she didn't think Mama wanted any more babies after Johnnie, but we both remembered her being sick in bed at times during the years following his birth, which caused us to speculate (much later on) that there'd been two, or possibly three, miscarriages before the little girls were born.

Mama sat quietly at her end of the table, watching plump little Kitty picking up crumbs from the tray of her high chair, and I remember thinking how pretty she looked in her light summer dress. I hoped we'd get home from the boat trip early enough so she'd have time to rest before going out with Papa. He did so love to show her off in one of the elaborate evening ensembles he could now afford to give her, and I didn't blame him. In spite of all the pregnancies, she'd kept her figure, and when she took the time to arrange her long copper-colored hair in the latest style, she looked almost regal. The hardships endured during the early years of marriage had left no visible scars whatsoever.

Nothing more was said about the boat trip that warm June evening. But the next morning when I came downstairs, Papa, who often breakfasted earlier than the rest of the family, was straightening his necktie at the mirror in the front hall, preparing to leave for the office.

"Take good care of your mother today, Maudie," he said softly when he saw me. "Don't let her overdo. That's a good girl. I know I can count on you. Angie may be the beauty, but you're the smart one."

He patted me affectionately on the shoulder, and a moment

15

later he was gone, leaving behind a faint scent of the Lilac Vegetal he rubbed on his face after shaving. I stood in the doorway watching him as he strode toward Fourth Avenue, a tall straight figure with a suggestion of a spring in his walk. I was just beginning to pay attention to men's looks, and I thought my father was more than merely presentable. His hair was black like mine, but straight and therefore more manageable, and his eyes were a *good* blue, almost as dark as Angie's. He had regular features and would have been handsome if it hadn't been for the scar that ran across the bridge of his nose, the result of some long-ago accident on a construction site.

He had fine-looking parents, I thought, and they must have been well off at one time since they sent him to the university in Dublin in the hope that he would become a lawyer.

"I was never cut out for the law," he said when Angie asked him why he had not done so. "I couldn't abide the thought of spending my life with all those dusty books and all the legal talk. That's all the law ever seemed to me—talk, talk, talk, argue, argue, and counterargue. And then there was your mother. If I had taken that road, it would have been years and years before I could afford to marry her. And nothing was going to stop me from doing that! Nothing!

"It's worked out, too. Ireland's always been a poor country, and at the end of my second year at the university, times were bad, very bad. Money was tight, and the old folks weren't sorry to see me emigrate to make my way in the New World. 'Twas a good time to come here too, with plenty of opportunity for anyone willing to work hard. New York was growing—it still is—and construction the business to be in. Matt Bailey, rest his soul, knew that, and I knew it, but it wasn't easy. It was damn hard work, and you boys better learn right now that if you want to be successful, you'll have to work harder than ever you thought you could. Success is not going to be handed to you, and don't you ever forget that.

"Well, it was nearly two years before I could send for your mother, and when I did, I spent weeks praying she'd have a safe crossing, not like the one I had. We ran into storm after storm, and more than half the people on board were either sick or dying. Two men were washed overboard in the heavy seas—it doesn't bear thinking about . . ."

So that's why he's so set against the trip today, I thought as I lingered on the sunny stoop. He's terrified of boats and water. . . .

"Maudie! Will you please stop daydreaming and come to breakfast?" Mama sounded impatient. "We'll not be ready in time if you dawdle so."

We were ready, though, and with time to spare. By eight-fifteen that bright June morning, Mama, Johnnie, the twins, and I were on the Recreation Pier at East Third Street, carrying lunch hampers, sweaters, sunshades, even an umbrella, and watching the *General Slocum* sail under the Williamsburg Bridge on its approach to the dock. It was a splendid sight—huge paddle wheels, tall smokestacks, and freshly painted decks all shining in the sunlight. The twins were in a state of high excitement, craning their necks to have a better view and already planning a game of hide-and-seek among the lifeboats. Johnnie stood quietly, one hand in mine and the other clutching the book he'd brought along. "In case I get bored with the scenery," he said.

We needn't have hurried. It was almost a quarter to ten before the boat took off, with a German band playing and everyone singing "A Mighty Fortress Is Our God." As I looked around, I could see Pastor Haas moving among his flock, smiling, shaking hands, and petting children. I had met him several times when we lived on Eleventh Street; he'd been a frequent visitor at the Bosenhart house, as I had been until we moved uptown. I doubted that he would remember me, though.

Mama, Johnnie, and Mrs. Bosenhart had settled themselves comfortably in the main cabin, and I was out on the deck with Elsie Bosenhart, trying to keep the twins in sight, when a woman standing near me said she smelled smoke. A member of the crew overheard her and said with a laugh that it was only the clam chowder boiling over in the galley.

We didn't know it then—I heard this much later—but a fire *had* started in a storage cabin down low in the vessel, and because of the way the ship was constructed, the smoke, accompanied by flames, traveled below the decks, unseen by anyone.

At that time an insane asylum was located on Sunken Meadow Island, and as we sailed past it I saw the inmates jumping up and down and gesturing wildly at us. Thinking they were just poor unfortunate crazy people, I waved back to them. A few minutes later I noticed a large number of ships that seemed to be headed in our direction, converging upon us, and before I had time to wonder what was going on, shouts and screams of "Fire! Fire!" split the air.

Curls of smoke were everywhere before tongues of flame burst through the deck we were on. I saw a panic-stricken crew member peel off his jacket and jump overboard, and moments later two little girls, their dresses on fire, followed him. A woman with an infant clutched to her breast pushed me to one side and climbed over the rail. I spotted Johnnie trying to reach a life jacket that hung on the outer wall of the cabin and started toward him, but I was immediately caught in a stampede of terrified passengers making for the stern, away from the flames that were enveloping the bow. I tried to push my way through the crowd to one of the lifeboats, hoping that the twins were in it and that they'd be lowered to safety, but I could make no progress. I turned to look once more for Johnnie and saw with relief that Mama had found him and held him in her arms. When I attempted to wave to her, several frantic passengers pinned me against the ship's railing screaming, "Jump, jump!"

Seconds later, the railing gave way, and I felt myself falling, falling . . .

IV

I remember very little about the next few days. I was sick, I was in a hospital—that much I knew since I was in a large room with several beds lined up on either side of a central aisle—but I had no recollection of how I had arrived there. I lay in bed drifting in and out of sleep, conscious from time to time of someone leaning over me and lifting my eyelids. I suppose I was bathed and fed, but I don't remember that. I couldn't see very well. Images were blurred, out of focus, and it seemed easier just to keep my eyes closed. I'm not sure how long that went on, and I didn't try to change things until I was coaxed into doing so.

"No response yet, Nurse?" I heard a male voice ask softly as a gentle hand touched my forehead.

"None, Dr. Cavanaugh," was the equally soft reply.

"It better be soon," the male voice murmured. "Let me try."

He took my hand in his—how comforting that felt!—and he, or someone, sat on the side of the bed.

"Can you hear me, honey? If you can, squeeze my hand—good girl! Now, try to speak; tell me your name. You can do it."

I knew my name, I was sure I knew my name, but I had trouble forming the words. I remember thinking how fortunate I was to have a short name; it wouldn't take so long to say. Somehow or other I managed to whisper what I thought was "Maud," but evidently it didn't come out right.

"I saw your lips move, honey, but I couldn't hear you. Try once more."

I wanted him to stay there holding my hand in his large warm one and thought if I could only say my name, he might not go away, but I guess I failed because I heard him say to the nurse that he'd be back later. I don't know how much time elapsed before he returned, but I must have been waiting for him to come because the moment I heard his voice, my eyes flew open. I could see clearly what I thought was the kindest, most wonderful face in the world looking down at me.

"I'm Maud Evans," I said out loud, and had just time enough to see the delight in his eyes before he leaned over and kissed me on the forehead.

I do not want to go into all the details of my recovery. Suffice it to say that it was a slow process and that it was a long time before I was told what had happened to me. The doctor, who said to call him Dr. Tom, came at least once, sometimes twice a day and monitored my progress. For a while my only concern was for myself, for getting through each day and pleasing him by eating everything given me and doing what I was told, but as I improved and my mind became clear, I found I could remember my family, my home, everything about my life up to the moment I fell into the river. I desperately wanted to see Mama and couldn't understand why she hadn't come to visit me. I remembered how she'd gone every single day to see Robbie when he was in the hospital. He'd been knocked down right in front of our house on Eleventh Street when the driver of a brewery wagon lost control of his team of horses. And I also wanted to know what had made me so sick.

I was frightened too. Was I going to die? At least half a dozen times during my hospital stay nurses would hurry into the ward carrying a screen, which they would set up around one of the beds. They would be followed by two orderlies wheeling a stretcher down the aisle, and a few minutes later a body, carefully covered with a gray blanket, would be removed from the room. Not a word was spoken. The hush that fell over the ward on those occasions was even more unnerving than the moans and cries of pains with which we lived.

At first no one would answer my questions, but eventually Dr. Tom told me I'd had a concussion. "You were unconscious when someone—I don't know who it was—pulled you out of the water. Could have been one of the patients here— the ambulatory ones were helping to rescue people. You evidently hit your head on something, part of the boat or a floating log. But you're recovering nicely, and we'll be sending you home in another week."

"But why doesn't Mama come?" I asked. "Or Angie?"

"They can't come here, honey," he answered gravely. "This is a hospital for infectious diseases, and no visitors are allowed. I know how tiresome it is here in the ward, Maud, but it won't be for much longer. Here, look—I've brought you a book to help pass the time. It's a new one, and I think you'll like it."

Then, with a warm smile and a gentle pat on my head, he turned and strode quickly down the aisle between the beds and out into the other parts of the hospital that I had never seen. I couldn't help but feel cheered by the thought of going home soon, home to Mama and my own bed in the room I shared with Angie where no one would groan or cry out in the night.

I just hoped Papa wouldn't be cross at me for falling into the water.

I picked up the book Dr. Tom had brought, *Beverly of Graustark,* but I couldn't concentrate on it. My head ached slightly, and as the day wore on, I felt increasingly miserable.

I don't want to think about the next two weeks. In fact, I can't remember much about them, but I know that in spite of all the good care I'd been given, I contracted the scarlet fever and for the second time in a month nearly died. For a while I felt so weak and wretched that I didn't care about anything. It was only when I discovered that my hair, which had all fallen out during the fever, began to grow back that I took any interest in recovering.

At first they wouldn't let me have a mirror. I guess they didn't want me to see how awful I looked, but finally Dr. Tom sent for one. I was astonished to see that I was almost pretty, that my freckles were gone, and instead of the unruly black mop I had never liked, I now had a neat little cap of soft light-brown hair, still rather short but showing signs of curling slightly at the ends.

Ah, vanity, vanity . . .

V

At the end of what I had come to think of as the longest eight weeks of my life, I was discharged from the hospital on August 15, in clothes Dr. Tom brought to me.

"I've no idea what happened to the clothes you were wearing when you were brought in, Maud," he said. "There probably wasn't much left of them, anyway. My sister has a daughter about your age, so I asked her to pick out some things for you. I thought she'd do a better job than I would."

I gasped when I opened the box and lifted out the dainty lavender voile dress, with trimmings of white braid, from its bed of tissue paper. It was the kind of dress I'd begged Mama to let me have, but she thought I was still too young for anything so sophisticated. Underneath, wrapped in more tissue paper, was a small pile of silky underthings, but I was too shy to unfold them in front of a man, even a doctor. Instead, I held the dress up to me and saw him smile and nod approvingly.

"Just the right color for your new head of hair, honey. Go ahead and put it on, and then I'll take you to a cab."

"Can't Mama even come to bring me home?" I asked.

"Afraid not, Maud," he answered, turning away and busying himself with the chart of the woman in the bed next to mine. "Now run along and get ready. I'll wait for you here."

I was puzzled by his tone. It wasn't like Dr. Tom to speak so abruptly to me, or to anyone for that matter, but I was too excited about leaving the hospital to let it bother me for more than a moment. The new clothes fitted me quite well, but the overall effect was somewhat marred by my footwear. Dr. Tom hadn't brought shoes, so I had to make do with a pair of worn felt slippers one of the nurses found for me. I don't think he noticed my feet, though. When I returned from the little dressing cubicle at one end of the ward, he simply took my hand and led me into a main hallway.

He rode with me on the ferry boat that ran between North Brother Island and the mainland (I think he was worried that I'd be afraid of any kind of boat), and when he handed me into a waiting hansom cab, he said he'd already paid the driver and that I was to sit back and enjoy the ride. "I'm going to miss you, honey," he said, "but I'm not going to say 'Come back and see us.' Perhaps I'll call on you sometime on my day off."

With that, he gave my shoulder one last reassuring pat and told the driver to go ahead. We started off, and when I looked back, he was hurrying toward the ferry boat with the long stride I had come to know so well. I was hoping he'd turn and wave, but just then we went around a corner, and I could no longer see him.

When we drew up in front of the house on Thirty-second Street, I asked the driver to wait while I went inside to find some money for a tip.

"Oh, no need, miss," he said cheerfully as he helped me down. "The doctor took care of that, he did."

Papa will have to send a check to Dr. Tom at the hospital

for the fare and for the clothes, I thought as I mounted the steps, if we can figure out how much. . . .

It was by no means the homecoming to which I had looked forward with such anticipation. When the door opened in answer to my ring, I looked at the man who stood there and I thought I was in the wrong house.

"Maudie, is it you?" he asked in a voice I barely recognized. "What the devil have you done to your hair? Come in, girl! Don't stand there gawking as if you didn't know your own father!"

I lowered my eyes, suddenly afraid of the man who stared at me. Everything about him—the unkempt black hair streaked with gray, the disgusting stubble on his face, and the hoarse, rasping voice—seemed to belong to a rough day laborer rather than the well-groomed, fastidious father I had known. Worst of all, I think, was the strong smell of whiskey he exuded instead of the delicate whiff of Lilac Vegetal.

"Mama—where is she?" I asked as a child began to cry somewhere in the house.

Without answering, he turned away and held on to the newel post as he shouted up the stairs. "Angie! Angie! Where the devil are you? Can't you stop all the caterwauling up there?"

He let go of the newel post and, swaying slightly, shuffled his way into the parlor. At that moment Angie came to the top of the stairs with a whimpering Megan tugging at her skirt, and the anguished look on my sister's face shocked me as much as if not more than my father's appearance. Tears were streaming down her cheeks by the time I reached her and hugged her to me. After a moment or two, Kitty came out of the nursery clamoring for attention, and Angie drew away from me.

"Angie, where's Mama? The twins? And what's the matter with Papa?"

"You don't know, do you, Maudie," she said softly.

"When the doctor telephoned, I told him not to tell you, but I wasn't sure whether he did or not. Maybe I should have let him, but he said you'd been so sick . . ."

"Tell me what, Angie? What has happened to everyone? Tell me! Is Mama sick?"

She shook her head, and after wiping her eyes led me into our bedroom. She gave the little ones a box of trinkets to keep them amused, then turned to face me. "Sit down, Maud," she said quietly, "and listen to me. You'll have to know now. Mama's gone, Maudie. She and the twins and Johnnie died in the fire on that boat. Papa hasn't been the same since. He won't go to the office, won't even answer the telephone when they call."

"Mama? Gone?" I stared at Angie, unable at first to grasp what she was saying. "She can't be. I saw her holding Johnnie—"

"She died, Maudie—"

"No, not Mama, not Mama, not Mama," I kept repeating until Angie put her arms around me and held me while I stared vacantly across the room. We sat on the bed, not speaking, not moving, until Kitty struggled up from the floor and said she wanted her lunch.

I went through the rest of the day like a sleepwalker. I have no memory of what went on. When I was getting ready for bed, however, my glance fell upon the quilted case Mama had made for my nightgown, and I burst into tears. It was a long time before I slept that night.

Later, much later, I learned that more than a thousand had perished in the *Slocum* disaster, primarily women and children, since the outing had taken place on a Wednesday when most of the fathers and husbands were at work. Pastor Haas had survived, but he had lost his wife and children, along with the majority of the parishioners of St. Mark's Church. My mother's body had washed up on the shore near Hunts Point in the Bronx, and the remains of the twins were later found in the buckets of the paddle wheels where they had gone to escape the flames. Poor Johnnie's body was never recovered. It may have been one of those burned beyond identification and buried in a large common grave in Queens Village, Long Island.

Angie said that Papa had been able to keep his emotions under control until the three coffins were lowered into the ground, but after that he simply abandoned himself to the despair that overwhelmed him.

In a way, it was fortunate that I had so little time to brood over my mother's death or allow myself the luxury of grief the way Papa did. During the days following my return from the hospital, Angie and I had our hands full. I'll never know how she had managed on her own. Papa was our biggest problem. Except for a daily trip to the saloon over on Third Avenue, he did not leave the house, spending the rest of the day in the parlor drinking and muttering to himself, complaining that he had nothing to live for, no wife, no sons to carry on his name, nothing but a houseful of girls. That was bad enough, but much worse were the occasions when he would get into a drunken rage and hurl imprecations upon the Knickerbocker Steamship Company, Captain Van Schlaick, the Lutheran church, and anything or anybody else connected with the ill-fated boat trip. It was because of these outbursts, Angie told me, that Tillie and Mrs. Murphy had left. Lizzie, the laundress, simply stopped coming.

"I couldn't blame them," she said, shaking her head ruefully. "They were frightened to death. One night he picked up a bowl of soup and threw it across the dining room, nearly hitting Mrs. Murphy. And I haven't dared hire anyone else. I'm afraid . . ."

"Afraid of what?" I asked.

"Of what he might do. Oh, there are plenty of maids and cooks to be had, but I doubt that anyone would put up with his actions. And then there's the money, Maudie. Where is it coming from now that he doesn't go to the office? We'll run out of it, and then what on earth will we do? Look at what he spends on whiskey! It's all he thinks about! Oh, I wish he'd drink himself to death before there's nothing left! I hate him! I hate him!"

She threw herself down on the bed and beat her fists against the pillow in an uncharacteristic display of temper that worried me almost as much as my father's behavior.

I am sure we could have settled down to manage the cooking, laundry, housework, and the care of two-year-old Megan and three-year-old Kitty easily enough if we hadn't been constantly worried about what Papa might do next. We kept out of his way as much as possible, but there were times when we couldn't avoid him. I remember how I dreaded asking him for money for groceries and how I would put it off until we were practically out of food. He'd stare at me angrily, as if I had no right to make such a request, and then lecture me on extravagance before taking out his purse and giving me a few dollars. "Make this last the week at least," he'd say as he thrust the bills at me.

I had never been interested in cooking, but fortunately Angie had, and somewhere along the line either Mama or Mrs. Murphy had taught her more than just the rudiments. She also knew how to shop, which cuts of meat to buy, how to wheedle a marrowbone out of the butcher (one of her smiles would usually accomplish this) and get him to throw in the soup greens for nothing. We ate a lot of soup those days—soup, potatoes, and applesauce—a diet Papa would have sneered at when Mama was alive, but since he was drinking so heavily, he had little interest in food. In fact, as Angie had said, he had little interest in anything but his whiskey. He seemed to live for nothing else.

In good weather we escaped from the house as often as we could, taking the little girls in their strollers for long walks through the quiet residential streets of the East Side, sometimes going as far north as Central Park. It was on those walks that we'd talk about our difficulties and cast about for solutions. Angie was so tired at night that she'd go to sleep as soon as we put out the light, but I would lie awake for a while, crying quietly.

We could think of no relatives to whom we might appeal for help. Mama's only sister had died years ago, and her husband had gone off to look for gold in the West. About Papa's family we knew next to nothing, only that his parents had died in a great famine and that he'd had two brothers, Tim and Sean. What had become of them we never heard.

"We're on our own, Maudie," Angie said one lovely cool afternoon in late September as we wheeled the children past the J. P. Morgan mansion and its gardens on Madison Avenue. The touch of fall in the air reminded me that the school year would be beginning and that I would have no part in it. There was no question of my returning to Miss Lawlor's Academy, for two reasons: Angie desperately needed my help, and Papa would undoubtedly refuse to pay the fees.

I was thinking that I was caught in a trap from which I could not extricate myself when I heard Angie's voice echoing my thought: "We're trapped, Maudie! And I don't know what to do! Papa's such a beast! If only he were himself again—if only he'd see a doctor! We can't go on like this—"

"You know he won't have anything to do with doctors, Angie, unless—"

"Unless what?"

"Unless we asked Dr. Sullivan to stop in—saying nothing to Papa."

Angie dismissed the idea immediately. "He'd slam the door in the doctor's face," she said contemptuously, "just the way he did when Larry McGuire called the last time. That was just after the funeral. He'd come to offer his condolences."

"You could elope with Larry," I said. "Then you'd be a married woman with your own home and your own children."

"Don't be daft! How could you think such a thing, Maudie. Larry's not rich at all, and besides, I swear I'll never have children. I've had enough of babies to last me the rest of my life. Come on, we'd better turn back. It's almost five o'-clock."

We walked back slowly, reluctant to exchange the serenity of the early fall day for whatever awaited us on the other side of our threshold. Things were quiet that day, though. Papa was morose but not cantankerous, and he ate most of the dinner Angie had prepared while I bathed the little ones. He spoke to neither of us during the meal and went straight back to the parlor after he pushed his plate away. He was still there when we went up to bed. Sometimes he stayed there all through the night.

It was the next day that he went too far. I was in the kitchen washing up the breakfast dishes and keeping an eye on Kitty and Megan when I heard Angie scream. She had just carried a tray in to Papa, who had not come to the table. I picked up Megan and, taking Kitty by the hand, hurried through the dining room and the short hall to the front of the house.

The parlor was a shambles. The little piecrust table, one of Mama's treasures, was overturned, and the contents of Angie's tray were scattered across the carpet. At first neither of them saw us as we stood in the doorway. He was standing in front of the fireplace, holding an empty bottle and shouting that someone had been at his whiskey.

Angie, her eyes blazing, held one hand to her face as she backed slowly away from him. "You hit me!" she cried. "You disgusting, filthy, drunken beast! If you ever do it again, I'll—"

Papa moved toward her, shifting the bottle in his hand so that he was holding it by the neck, as if he intended to swing it at her.

"Angie!" I screamed. "Look out! He's going to—"

The sound of my voice distracted him, and when he turned to look at me, Angie picked up the straight chair that Mama had kept alongside the table. Holding it by its back, she thrust the four legs into Papa's chest and stomach with more force than I would have thought possible. He fell backward, landing heavily on the floor with his head against one of the firedogs that held the grate for the coal, and lay still.

No one moved for a moment or two. Then Kitty began to cry. Megan wriggled down from my arms and picked up a piece of toast from the floor.

Angie felt his pulse. "He's dead," she said in a whisper. "And I killed him!"

"It was an accident, Angie," I said. "You only meant to keep him from hitting you with the bottle—"

"But the police—"

"We'll say he fell—which is the truth. Put the chair back, but leave the mess on the floor. He was drunk. He knocked the table over, and then he fell. It wasn't your fault. . . ."

"No, it wasn't, was it. I know I've said I could kill him, but, Maudie, you know I never would have—"

"Of course I know that. Now we'd better telephone. I'll call Dr. Sullivan first."

VI

For days after Papa's death, weeks even, our lives seemed to stand still, as if we were suspended in some strange limbo waiting for something, an event or a person, to bring us back to reality. I refer to Angie and me, of course. Kitty and Megan were too young to understand what had happened.

Now as I look back, though, perhaps I was the only one who felt as if the world had stopped. Angie went about her daily activities in a thoughtful, determined way, and the only change I noticed in her was that as time went on she became less communicative, giving me the impression that she was withdrawing from me and becoming lost in some secret place of her own.

The authorities, medical and legal, never questioned our statement that Papa had fallen while drunk. The fact that the empty whiskey bottle was still clutched in his right hand when they examined him lent credence to our story. We both denied seeing him fall.

Angie said she had placed the tray of tea and toast on the

piecrust table and returned to the kitchen. He'd been sprawled in his big armchair, she said, and had only grunted when she spoke to him. No, she didn't know how much he'd been drinking, but there were more than a dozen empty bottles in the chest beneath the window.

No, I didn't have anything to add to what she said. I'd been in the kitchen taking care of our younger sisters.

The police did not subject us to prolonged questioning, and the interview was shorter than I had expected. The doctor signed the death certificate—"accidental death while under the influence of alcohol"—and the lawyer said he would see that our father's will was probated. Two days later, Papa was buried next to the graves of Mama and the twins, and as I watched the coffin being lowered into the ground, I could not help but wonder what kind of punishment or retribution would be meted out to Angie and me. There was no doubt in my mind that she was responsible for his death and that I had perjured myself to protect her.

Apparently Papa's affairs were in a jumble, and it seemed to take forever for the estate to be settled. In the meantime, the executor made us a small monthly allowance, not sufficient for luxurious living but enough so that we were able to hire an Irish girl, Kathleen O'Rourke, to help with the housework and the care of Kitty and Megan. Also, when we were going through Papa's things, getting his clothes ready to give to the St. Vincent de Paul Society, we were surprised to find a little box in the top bureau drawer under his handkerchiefs that contained almost five hundred dollars in cash.

"For his whiskey," Angie said bitterly.

We didn't mention the money to the lawyer.

There were times when I thought Angie was becoming restless and wondered if she might be feeling remorseful or guilty

34

about Papa. We never talked about what happened that morning; she didn't bring it up, and I was afraid to mention it. I tried to put it out of my mind, but for weeks afterward I couldn't go past the parlor door without picturing him sprawled on the floor. Angie may have been having the same trouble.

Not too long after Papa's death, maybe six weeks or so, young men, Lester Elmendorf and Larry McGuire among them, began to call on Angie again. She received them graciously in the parlor, although somewhat coolly, I thought. She accepted their offerings of flowers and chocolates but refused to go out with them on the grounds that it would not be proper for her to be seen in public so soon after her father's death.

I suspected that that was not her real reason for declining their invitations. After all, she had hated Papa passionately, and any show of respect for his memory was nothing if not hypocrisy. But Angie was no hypocrite.

She waited until one cold afternoon in mid-December to tell me what was on her mind. We were out shopping for toys for Kitty and Megan, and after we'd found a doll for each one, a jack-in-the-box and a few other little things, Angie led the way into a specialty shop on the Ladies' Mile, one that Mama had gone to for material for evening dresses.

"You look puzzled, Maudie," she said as we left the shop carrying heavy parcels of blue crèpe de chine and guipure lace, "but don't worry—I know what I'm doing." And she smiled to herself.

"Are you going out someplace with Larry McGuire?" I asked.

"Yes, with him or Lester—no, not Lester—maybe with Dan Freeman or Alec Murchison. They can afford to spend more. But that's only part of it. I intend to marry well, Maudie, a man with enough money. I mean *real* money, inherited wealth, so there'll never be any question of being poor or having to make do and so you and Kitty and Megan will have enough. We were poor when we lived down on Eleventh Street, but we were young then and didn't know anything else. Now we do, and I do not intend to scrimp and save for the rest of my life. That's the reason for the new gown, you see."

"What about Mama's dresses?" I asked. "They're still in her closet, and one of them might fit you."

"Oh, don't be silly, Maudie! They're lovely, but they were made for an older woman. If I wore one of them, I'd look just like a girl in her mother's old dress. I need my own gown, and I shall ask to be taken to the best restaurants, the opera, the theater, a *box* in the theater. *The Merry Widow* is playing at the New Amsterdam. I won't meet any rich men if I'm not seen in the right places.

"Don't look so appalled, Maudie!" she exclaimed after glancing at me. "I may sound mercenary, but I'm just using the wits God gave me. I've a feeling Papa's estate won't amount to much. The lawyer said something about the debts that would have to be paid before we could expect anything, and who knows how much Papa owed? Remember how he refused to answer the phone? He probably knew it was someone he owed money to. We may get nothing, and then how could we pay the rent?

"We'd both have to go to work, and what are we trained for? And who would take care of the children? We'd have to live in a tenement—awful places they are, too. Remember the time Mama sent us down to Clarkson Street to buy some artificial flowers from the poor family she'd heard about?"

I remembered it clearly. The mother and father and three young children were sitting around a wooden table in the most primitive kitchen I'd ever seen. The parents fashioned the flowers while the young ones wrapped green paper around the wire stems, all by the dim light of a single oil lamp. There wasn't even a window in the room. Water dripped from a broken faucet, the oven door hung open on a rusty hinge, and a line of drying clothes stretched across everything. We bought the flowers and took them home, but Mama threw them out after hearing our description of the place.

"You see the danger we're in, don't you, Maudie?" Angie asked as we turned the corner into Thirty-second Street.

I nodded, but more clearly than any financial danger I could see that nothing was going to deter Angie from pursuing the course she had outlined. I wasn't happy about it, but who was I to object when she seemed to have my welfare, and that of Kitty and Megan, at heart?

For the next few weeks Angie devoted herself to preparations for her appearance in society. Miss Fessenton, the seamstress Mama had used, took over the empty master bedroom, and the old Singer sewing machine, the kind one worked by pumping a pedal up and down, hummed from morning to night. Besides the blue evening gown, Angie was having a rather elaborate afternoon dress made ("in case I'm invited to tea at the Fifth Avenue Hotel"). It was a lovely creation of navy-and-white striped surrah with silk fringe and lingerie flowers.

And the hats! She couldn't decide whether a small toque, simply trimmed, or a broad-brimmed sailor would best complement the afternoon dress. In the end she bought both, as well as a picturesque Gainsborough straw hat that was worn tilted on one side of the head. I didn't know when she expected to wear this last one—probably with still another dress, the long diaphanous one she'd been talking about. I was pretty sure that most if not all of the five hundred dollars in Papa's box went for these outfits, but I did not ask.

The Christmas preparations were left almost entirely to me; Angie was far too engrossed in expanding her wardrobe to be of any help. There wasn't, however, very much to do; I bought a small tree and let Megan and Kitty hand me the old-fashioned hand-carved angels and animals that had hung on every tree we'd ever had. Mama once told me she'd bought them for a penny each from a poor cripple on the Bowery.

On Christmas Eve, after I'd filled two small stockings with miniature toys and arranged the few larger ones under the tree, I sat alone in the parlor for a few minutes, thinking that it all looked rather pathetic in comparison with previous Christmases. I was close to tears at that point and probably would have given in to them if Angie hadn't called me upstairs to help her hook her dress, the one she was planning to wear to a New Year's ball at the Astor House. Somehow or other, she had persuaded Larry McGuire to buy tickets for it. Poor Larry . . .

VII

Of the four or five young men who were courting Angie, only Lester Elmendorf balked at the extravagant demands she made. Perhaps he suspected her of having ulterior motives and decided he would not be used. And for all I know, the others may have gone without lunch to take her to the theater and expensive restaurants. I've often wondered if they weren't somehow relieved when she accepted a wealthy suitor.

Whatever her strategy was, it worked well, and by the late spring of 1905 she was engaged to Derek Blauvelt, a man twice her age (she was eighteen). He came from an old New York family of Dutch ancestry and had succeeded his father as head of Blauvelt and Company, a Wall Street firm that dealt in foreign exchange and investment. He had, in Angie's words, "untold wealth."

"It was really very easy, Maudie," she said with a laugh as she held out her hand so that I could admire the diamond that glistened in the sunlight. "I first saw him looking at me at the opera, and later, when we were having supper at Sherry's, I could *feel* him watching me. But he didn't approach me that night; he's far too well bred to do anything so crass. I don't think Alec noticed him. He kept *his* eyes on me."

I was not surprised at that. Angie had looked incredibly beautiful the night Alec Murchison took her to hear Caruso sing. The blue crêpe de chine gown, cut low in front and trimmed with the guipure lace at the neckline, emphasized the slenderness of her waist and the soft curves of her figure. She wore no jewelry, not even Mama's pearls. She needed none. Those deep blue eyes sparkled with anticipation, and beneath the softly piled shining hair her complexion fairly glowed. A pair of long kid gloves, the kind that come up above the elbow, and Mama's dark-blue velvet evening cloak, expertly altered by Miss Fessenton, completed her costume. Oh yes—and high-heeled satin slippers. It was no wonder Alec Murchison couldn't take his eyes off her.

When I asked her how Derek Blauvelt managed an introduction to her, her reply was vague—something about a mutual acquaintance presenting him. She was beginning to keep her own counsel more and more as time went on, volunteering only what she wanted me to hear.

I was not particularly impressed by what I saw of her fiancé. He struck me as polite enough but somewhat cold, and although he wasn't ugly, no one would ever call him handsome. He was of medium height, only about an inch or two taller than she, and on the whole rather colorless, with his already thinning light-blond hair and pale-gray eyes. He couldn't compare with Larry McGuire as far as looks went.

"He'll give me anything I want, Maudie," Angie said one evening as I watched her dress for dinner with Derek. "I've explained that arrangements will have to be made for you and the little ones, and he's agreed to pay the rent here and make you a monthly allowance. I don't think he'll ever want to have you live with us, but don't worry—we'll still see lots of each other."

She was wrong there: after the wedding in the fall of 1905, I saw very little of Angie and less of Derek. When they returned from their honeymoon in Europe, my sister was so caught up in her new activities that she had little time to spare us. I gathered that Derek expected her to fill the place once occupied by his mother on the boards of various charitable organizations (I was sure she hated that) and to devote her evenings to the social events he deemed worthy of his presence.

"I don't know where the time goes, Maudie," she said on one of her infrequent visits to Thirty-second Street. "I hardly have a moment to myself. If it isn't one board meeting full of stuffy old ladies and gentlemen, it's another one. To the Blauvelts, philanthropy is a sacred duty. And the dinner parties! Some days I scarcely have time to change my clothes, let alone tend to the fittings for new outfits. Derek doesn't like to see me wear the same dress too often. . . ."

"Are you happy, Angie?" I asked when she paused for breath.

She looked at me in surprise for a moment, then laughed. "Why of course I'm happy, you ninny," she said. "Why wouldn't I be? I have everything I want."

Perhaps she was happy, but if so, it was not a relaxed, comfortable happiness that emanated from her but something more brittle.

I wasn't particularly happy myself, although Angie had done her best to see that I had no worries. A sizable check was deposited on the first of each month to an account Derek had opened in my name, and while I was grateful for the security this provided, I could not help but feel resentful at being treated as a charity case. No, I was not happy, and I was lonely. I felt that I was simply putting in time, existing, without any purpose or goal, unlike Angie, who knew what she wanted and went after it. I had to smile when I thought of how Papa would have raved about the elegant town house on Fifth Avenue near Sixty-third Street and the large Blauvelt estate overlooking the Hudson above Tarrytown, both of which Derek had inherited from his parents. Would he have liked Derek, though? Probably not.

On occasion Angie would arrive at Thirty-second Street in the carriage Derek had given her and take the three of us for a ride through the park and then to tea at some small hotel. We never dined at the Fifth Avenue house. I could understand that they might not want the children at their formal table, but they might have invited me. Then in the summer of 1906 Angie did take the three of us to the house on the Hudson for a week when Derek was away on business. Perhaps he simply did not like having children around. . . .

Papa's estate had been settled by that time, and as Angie had suspected, most of it went to pay his creditors, leaving us with a little over a thousand dollars in cash. If Derek had not subsidized us, and I must say he was extremely generous, I don't know how I would have managed. Later on, however, it occurred to me that it might have been better for me if he hadn't supported us. I would have had to go to work sooner than I did and wouldn't have frittered away three years of my life.

By the fall of 1907 I was eighteen and still at loose ends, longing for some activity other than managing a household (even with Kathleen O'Rourke to help, there was plenty for me to do) and being responsible for Kitty and Megan. They were good children, but like any normal, five- and six-year-olds, they demanded a good deal of attention, leaving me little time for myself.

I remember going to bed in tears one night in early September after a particularly trying weekend. Rain had kept us indoors both days, and I don't think the children stopped whining to go out from the time they woke up on Saturday morning until I got them to bed on Sunday night. It had been Kathleen's weekend off too.

Whether it was desperation, loneliness, or general dissatisfaction with the way things were that led me to take the step I did I cannot say, but on the Monday following that rainy weekend I enrolled both girls in Miss Lawlor's Private Academy on Thirty-seventh Street where Angie and I had gone. I told the headmistress to send the bill for their tuition to Angie, and then hurried up to Forty-second Street and enrolled myself in the Babcock Typewriter School (in those days the typist as well as the machine was known as a typewriter). I paid the fee out of the housekeeping funds, wondering what Derek would say if he knew—but then, he had never asked me for an accounting.

As I said earlier, we saw very little of my sister during the "season"; she was far too busy with her social life. By the time she found out what I was doing, I had become quite proficient at my machine and had mastered a few other secretarial skills like filing and the rudiments of bookkeeping, and was beginning to think of looking for employment. She was waiting for me when I arrived home at dusk one afternoon, and a glance at her face told me she was out of sorts.

"Kathleen told me what you are doing, Maud," she said crossly. "I don't believe Derek will be pleased—"

"Derek has nothing to say about it," I said sharply. "He does not run my life, or tell me what to do."

"He pays your expenses, and you owe him some consideration."

"If that's what's bothering you, Angie, put your mind at rest. As soon as I find a position, I'll return the money I borrowed from the housekeeping account to pay for the typewriter school. Anyway, I didn't think you and Derek cared what I did, as long as I kept out of your way! And kept Kitty and Megan—"

"Maudie! Haven't we provided for you? Haven't we given you—"

"Yes, you've clothed and fed us, and I suppose I should be grateful, but I'm through being dependent on you, Angie. I am no longer a child, and I will do as I please. You can tell Derek to keep his money. I plan to leave this house. You'll have to take Kitty and Megan."

"Oh, Derek won't stand for that!" she exclaimed. "Why are you acting like this, Maudie? Haven't we supplied you with—"

"With what I no longer want," I said angrily. "Now go and make arrangements for the children, Angie, because I mean what I say."

When she left a few minutes later, nothing was settled, but I could see that she was thoroughly frightened by my rebellion. No doubt she was worried about how her life would be affected.

I did not expect to hear from Angie immediately, but as the days stretched into weeks and I had no communication from her, I realized that she planned to do nothing about Kitty and Megan. She would bank on the fact that I would not walk out and leave them, which, of course, I wouldn't until I was sure she'd take them. Then, when Derek continued to deposit the monthly check at the Corn Exchange Bank, I came to the conclusion that she hadn't even mentioned our conversation to him. I wondered if she was afraid to bring it up.

In the meantime, quite by accident, I found a position. I was passing a bookstore on Lexington Avenue on my way to the bank when I noticed a sign in the window: TYPEWRITER WANTED. INQUIRE WITHIN. After hesitating for a moment, I pushed the door open, causing a bell to jingle.

Floor-to-ceiling shelves lined all the wall space, and the central portion of the room was crowded with tables of various sizes and shapes, each overflowing with books that looked far from new. An air of disorder, comfortable disorder, hung over the place, which I found rather pleasant, but I wondered how long it would take to locate a book for a customer.

At the moment, however, neither customer nor clerk was in evidence. I was beginning to feel that I had no right to stand there examining the place and was about to leave when a door at the rear of the store burst open.

A rotund little man bounced down the narrow aisle between the tables toward me. "Ah, good morning, good morning!" he called out. "Is there something special—have you been waiting long? I couldn't find some papers—oh, and no Danny! The lazy fellow must have overslept again! Oh, my, my—yes, my dear, what can I do for you? Name's Heimlich, by the way."

When I explained that I had seen his sign in the window and that I knew how to type, I think he was more pleased than if I'd come to buy a dozen books. Without hesitating a minute, he led me to the back of the store. When he opened the door to his office, standing back politely and waiting for me to enter, I was surprised by the coziness and warmth of the room in front of me.

I had never seen an office of any kind, but at the Babcock Typewriter School I had pictured a large impersonal room with rows of young women dressed in shirtwaists and dark skirts sitting on hard, uncomfortable chairs in front of their machines. Our classroom had been like that—a cold, dreary room, uncarpeted, and with bare walls painted a cheerless gray, so uninviting that more than once I wondered if I had chosen the right occupation.

My common sense should have told me that the bookseller's establishment couldn't possibly contain anything like the picture I had in my mind. Angie would have called me a ninny. In any case, I was delighted with what I saw. In comparison with the office I had envisioned, Mr. Heimlich's room was pure delight—messy, yes, but cozy. Cretonne curtains hung on either side of a sunny window, a faded Persian rug, patterned like the one in our dining room, covered most of the floor, and a large rolltop desk overladen with papers and books stood against one wall. A new Royal typewriter on its own sturdy table occupied the space between the window and the opposite wall, and the chair in front of it, I noted with approval, had an upholstered seat.

"I've been left in the lurch, my dear," Mr. Heimlich said with a laugh after giving me time to look around, "but not exactly at the church. Your predecessor ran off and married her young man. And just after I'd bought her this new machine! Ah well, I wish them joy. Going to Florida to grow oranges, she said. Now, here's the sort of thing you'll be doing. . . ."

I like to look back on the time I spent working for kind, cheerful Mr. Heimlich and remember his almost childish delight in the way I brought order to his haphazard filing system and kept his invoices and correspondence up to date.

"Why, now I can find things!" he'd say several times a week. "And so can Danny, the scribbler."

Danny was the only other employee. He stayed out in the shop proper waiting on customers, and when business was slow, as it often was, he'd climb up on a stool behind one of the shelves and work away at what he told me was his "opus magnum." If there should be a flurry of activity, he'd call me to come out into the store to help, but that wasn't until I'd been there long enough to familiarize myself with at least some of the stock.

Since I earned only eight dollars a week (Danny made ten),

I had second thoughts about leaving home and being independent of Derek. That would have to wait until I was earning more. I made a few inquiries at rooming houses in the neighborhood, but although they were probably perfectly respectable, I did not like the slatternly appearance of the maids who answered my ring or the cabbagey smell that seemed characteristic of all of them. Besides, the fee for board and lodging was between six and seven dollars a week, which would leave me practically penniless.

The thought of the austerity of such a life frightened me a little, and after a while I began to regret the rash declaration I had made to Angie. As time went on, however, and she made no move to take the children or to stop Derek's support, I simply waited, and every Saturday added another eight dollars to the growing pile of bills in a shoe box in my closet. I found satisfaction in being a wage earner. In fact, I was enjoying myself more than I had in a long time.

My expenses were few: I was close enough to Thirty-second Street to go home for the lunch Kathleen had ready for me, unlike poor Danny, who either ate a sandwich and an apple while he worked on his opus or, when he slept too late to prepare anything, went to the saloon on the corner for a five-cent glass of beer and whatever "free lunch" was to be had.

"The ham and sausage you can trust, Miss Evans," he said, "but keep away from the sauerkraut and pickled eggs; they've been there forever." As if I ever thought of going into a saloon.

Kathleen made things easy for me. She walked Kitty and Megan to school in the morning, met them in the afternoon, and took care of all the meals. She was a competent, uncomplaining young woman and seemed to enjoy being in charge of the household during my absence. Perhaps she felt as if she'd been promoted from housemaid to housekeeper. I hoped she wouldn't be in a hurry to marry the redheaded Irishman who called for her on her days off.

I couldn't see much chance of advancement at the bookstore, but only on rare occasions did I think about leaving and looking for more remunerative work. I was not only happily occupied, but after a conversation with one of the young women I'd known at the typewriter school, I realized how fortunate I'd been to find such convenient and congenial employment.

Lily Pease, a large girl who looked as if she'd be more suited to life on a farm than in the city, came into the store one Saturday afternoon when I was helping Danny with the customers. Inside of five minutes she convinced me that I had better stay where I was. "You're a lucky one, you are, Maud," she said, idly fingering a copy of Ellen Glasgow's *The Wheel of Life*. "Don't ever go near any of the big insurance companies! It's murder! All you do is bang away on an old machine from morning to night, turning out one stupid form after another—and all for seven a week! Slave labor, I call it. Here you at least have a chance to move around, to meet people. We might as well be chained to our machines. And who's there to meet in that place? No one but grubby salesmen flying in and out, ordering you to type this, type that, at once, at once! I wouldn't want one of them anyway. Oh well, maybe someday I'll find something else. Look, my dad gave me a dollar and a half to buy a book for my ma's birthday. What should I get? She likes the romantic stuff."

I sold her a copy of *The Awakening of Helena Ritchie*, and as I was wrapping it, she asked me to keep her in mind if I heard of a good job.

I watched her bustle out of the store, and when I turned around, Danny was grinning at me. "Makes you count your blessings, doesn't it, Miss Evans?" he asked in a soft voice before turning to another customer. He was right.

It became customary for me to take over in the shop while Danny had his lunch. Workers with ten or fifteen minutes to spare before going back to their offices would drop in, once in a while to buy a book but more often to browse among the piles on the tables. Danny told me he'd been watching one young man for over a month and swore that each day the fellow would read five or six pages of a novel until he finished it and then start another one.

It was on one of those noon hours that Larry McGuire came in, an older version of the boy who had courted Angie three years earlier. There was no sign of the hesitant youth who had appeared at our door with chocolates and flowers in the confident young man who walked quickly down one of the aisles toward me.

"I'm looking for—why, Maudie! It is you, isn't it? Good to see you!" he exclaimed as he shook my hand.

We chatted for a few minutes. He'd finished law school, he said, and was studying for the bar exam. He asked about Kitty and Megan but made no mention of Angie. I was conscious, though, that he watched me closely as I wrapped the book he bought. Was he looking for a resemblance to my sister? He'd been most attentive to her.

Of course, I didn't look anything like Angie, but by that time I was aware that my appearance had improved considerably. I was no longer painfully thin, and my second crop of hair was ever so much more attractive than the first one. I knew I was pretty, but I also knew that I could never compete with Angie in looks. Perhaps, as things turned out, it was just as well.

VIII

The events of the next two years, or at least a good many of them, make me shudder when something brings them to mind. I don't know why I *do* think about them. Maybe I can't help it when I see a certain blue flower or catch a glimpse of Megan in profile. At times, her resemblance to Angie is almost uncanny.

It all began when I arrived home from the bookstore a little after five on a cold evening in January 1908. When a worried-looking Kathleen met me at the door, my first thought was that something had happened to Kitty or Megan, that they'd been hurt, or kidnapped. "The children?" I asked anxiously.

"No, Miss Maud, it's not to do with them. They're fine, they are. I'm keeping them in the kitchen. It's Miss Angela— she's come, and the good Lord knows the matter with her. In your room, she is, carryin' on, cryin' her eyes out. . . ."

As I ran upstairs, still wearing my hat and coat, I could hear Angie moaning in a way that made me think she was in pain. She had thrown herself facedown on her old bed and didn't see me at first. As I stood in the doorway looking at her, she beat her fists against the pillow, just as she had the night she was so furious at Papa.

"Angie," I said softly, "what is it? What is wrong?"

Startled, she sat up and looked at me blankly. "Everything," she murmured after a moment. "You wouldn't understand. Everything's wrong—the whole world—oh, go away! Leave me alone!"

She lay quietly, no longer crying, but when she saw me still standing at the foot of the bed, she told me again to leave her alone and closed her eyes. I hesitated, then put a quilt over her and went downstairs to have dinner in the kitchen with the children.

"Why is Angie here?" Megan asked. "Why was she crying? Did she hurt herself?"

"Maybe she's hungry," Kitty suggested. To her, food was a sure remedy for almost any ailment.

"She'll eat something later," I said. "She's resting now, and you mustn't disturb her."

"Shall I be takin' a tray up to her, would you think?" Kathleen asked at the end of our meal.

"She ought to eat something, I suppose," I answered. "If you fix it, Kathleen, I'll take it up. I can just leave it if she's asleep."

"Give her some chocolate cake," Kitty advised. "A piece with lots of frosting on it."

I didn't think Angie would be interested in food just then, but the tray provided me with an excuse to approach her.

She was awake when I opened the door, lying on her back, staring at the ceiling. "Come in, Maudie," she said, waving the tray away. "You might as well hear the worst. I've left Derek. He threatened me with—oh, I don't know what I'm going to do!"

"Why on earth would he—"

"Oh, it doesn't matter why, does it?" she asked impatiently.

"It does matter, Angie. It sounds crazy."

"I think he is crazy, Maudie. No, not crazy—he's raging mad. I should have known better. . . ."

It took over an hour for me to get the story out of her, and even then I wasn't sure that I'd heard the whole story. Apparently Derek suspected her of having an affair—she wouldn't tell me the man's name—and hired a private detective to follow her. It seemed that Elliot Crenshaw, a member of Derek's club, had told him that his wife had seen Angie having tea with a certain man in the Park Hotel and had watched them enter an elevator together afterward.

Derek waited until he had a call from the detective before speaking to Angie. According to the man's report, Mrs. Blauvelt had dined twice with Mr. X while Mr. Blauvelt was in Washington for the better part of a week, and on both occasions the two had returned to the Fifth Avenue house in a cab. Mr. X took leave of Mrs. Blauvelt at the door and then strolled around the block two or three times before entering the house through the delivery entrance, to which he had a key. He did not emerge until dawn was breaking.

When Derek confronted Angie with the report, she denied everything, saying she hardly knew the man. She'd danced with him once or twice, but that was all.

"Cecelia Crenshaw is a nasty woman, Maudie, a troublemaker. She's jealous of my looks, I know, but Derek wouldn't believe me. He said I was making a fool of him, a cuckold, and that I'd besmirched the Blauvelt name as well as jeopardizing certain prospects of his in Washington. Nothing of this sort had ever happened in his family, he said, and he wasn't going to stand for it. Those old Blauvelts probably kept their women under lock and key," she finished bitterly.

"But *did* you have an affair, Angie?"

"Do you think I'm an idiot?" She glared at me and then looked away quickly. "It's all that Crenshaw woman's doing. She and Liza Fiske are as catty a pair as you'll ever see."

She talked on and on about how unfair Derek was, how he demanded too much of her, how jealous he was if she even spoke to another man, and how cross he became if she took more than one glass of champagne. "So I've left him, Maudie, and I came here because I wanted time to think about what to do. I had just enough money in my purse to pay for the cab. I don't know what I'm going to do for money now. Derek won't give me any more—I'm sure of that."

It didn't occur to her to wonder what the rest of us would do without Derek's support, not then at any rate, and I was too tired to think about trying to manage on my eight dollars a week. About midnight, I found a nightgown for her and told her we both needed sleep. I suddenly felt like the older sister, the one in charge, but as I lay in the dark room listening to Angie move about restlessly in the other bed, I found myself wishing Mama was there. I knew I was neither mature nor wise enough to deal with the situation Angie had created. I had no idea what steps, if any, I should take.

The problem of what to do next was suddenly taken out of my hands the next morning. I slipped out of the bedroom while Angie was still asleep, her cheek resting on the open palm of one hand, her long hair cascading over the pillow. After breakfast, when I was in the parlor helping Kitty with her arithmetic, Derek came. Megan answered his ring and after one terrified look at him hid behind the sofa. He'd never spoken a sharp word to her, but the expression on his face that morning was enough to frighten any child. I was startled myself, not so much by the severity of his appearance as by the unnatural brightness of his eyes, and found myself shrinking from him as he entered the room.

"I've come for Angela, Maud," he said in a surprisingly normal voice. "Has she arisen yet?" He spoke calmly, matter-of-factly, as if it were the most natural thing in the world for Angie to spend a night with us, but I noticed that he kept shifting his weight from one foot to the other and glancing nervously around the room.

"I don't think so," I answered. "I'll go upstairs and see—"

"No, no. Don't trouble yourself," he said quickly. "Just tell me which room she is occupying. No, don't come up: I'll see her alone."

The children and I watched him mount the stairs, and we heard a door open and close. After that the house was ominously still; even Kitty and Megan were quiet. My hands were cold, and as I tried to warm them over the fire, I could not rid myself of the thought that Derek had brought something evil into the house with him.

When he came downstairs half an hour later, he was holding Angie firmly by the arm. They paused in the front hall, and Derek thanked me for the hospitality I had shown his wife. Angie said nothing, nor did she look at me, and a moment later they were gone. I watched from the parlor window as he handed her into the waiting carriage, but she did not look back.

I tried to reach my sister by telephone several times during the weeks that followed her unsatisfactory visit, but on each occasion I was told that Mrs. Blauvelt was not at home, and the messages I left for her remained unanswered.

That winter, a particularly cold and stormy one, seemed endless, even though I began to "step out" a bit, as Kathleen put it. Larry McGuire invited me to have lunch or dinner with him a few times, and a friend of Danny's, a quiet, studious young man named James Mahoney, called frequently. There were a few others (not Angie's castoffs, either), and while I enjoyed the attention, it all seemed rather pointless. But that's completely irrelevant now.

As I said, it was a bad winter, and throughout the short gray days and the long dark nights I was seldom free of concern for my sister. She seemed to have vanished. I no longer came across items on the society page saying that among the guests of Mr. and Mrs. So-and-so were Mr. Blauvelt and the beautiful Mrs. Blauvelt. It occurred to me that they had gone abroad, but no one at the Fifth Avenue house would give me any information, and when I screwed up enough courage to phone Derek at the offices of Blauvelt and Company, I was told that he was out of town.

Then, in late May, when the weather had at last warmed up, I received a letter from Angie.

> *Blauvelt House*
> *Tarrytown, N.Y.*
> *May 11, 1908*

> *Dear Maudie,*
>
> *I don't know what you thought of me, going off without saying a word to you that morning last January. Please forgive me; I wasn't myself.*
>
> *I need to see you, and Derek has said that you and Kitty and Megan may come for a long visit this summer. Please say you'll come. Derek will make the travel arrangements.*
>
> *Love,*
>
> *Angie*
>
> *P.S. I think you also had better bring Kathleen O'Rourke to keep Kitty and Megan in order.*

I took my time replying to her. That a summer in the country would be good for the children I knew, but it would mean giving up my job, for one thing, and I was not at all certain that I wanted to spend several weeks in Derek's mansion, for another. On the other hand, Angie had written that she needed to see me. . . .

IX

I imagine that under normal circumstances a summer at Blauvelt House would be idyllic. The carefully tended gardens and
terraced lawn, the orchards with their ripening fruit, the acres
and acres of surrounding woodland with its trails, and especially the ever-changing moods of the Hudson—all should
have induced an atmosphere of tranquillity and gracious living.
Oh, the gracious living was there, at least on the surface, but
I was unable to ignore an air of gentle oppression (I can think
of no better word) that hovered over all that beauty.

At first I thought it was the quiet of that isolated spot in the
country that bothered me, the lack of the familiar noises of the
city. Occasional sounds from the riverboats were the only sign
of the outside world, and in spite of our proximity to the
water, the boats I watched gliding by seemed as remote as the
falling stars we saw from time to time.

The problem, I thought then, was Derek. His presence
could be felt everywhere, even when he was on one of his
frequent trips to New York or Washington. It was not a warm
presence, either, not the kind that encourages one to enjoy

life, but a cold, unwelcoming one that causes voices to be kept low and occupations to be carried on silently.

Those were the thoughts I had early in our visit. Later I changed my mind and decided that it was Mrs. Williams, the housekeeper, who set the tone. She was tall and angular, an unattractive woman who wore her straight black hair pulled back severely in a small bun. Everything about her was severe, from her narrow face with its pointed nose and small beady eyes to her long ringless fingers. I never saw her dress in anything but unrelieved black, but perhaps that was the proper apparel for a housekeeper. I thought the other servants—the cook, the chambermaids, the parlor maid, and the laundress—were afraid of her. I know I would have been had she been my superior.

I never heard a clatter of pots or dishes from the kitchen when meals were being prepared or the sound of furniture being moved across the floor when the rooms were being cleaned, but those things were done, and done to perfection. Once I heard one of the maids giggling in the pantry, but that was all.

I doubt that Mrs. Williams had any authority over the men on the staff—the gardener, the grooms, or the stableboy. But I noticed that they kept out of her way. James, the head groom and chauffeur who lived with his wife in a cottage near the stables, drove the housekeeper into town several mornings a week, but I doubt that that large ruddy-faced Irishman stood in awe of anyone, even the dour Mrs. Williams.

I must admit that she ran Derek's household competently, but it was all a bit eerie, and several times I found myself escaping with Kathleen and the children to the meadow beyond the orchard where the world seemed more natural. Kitty and Megan thrived in the country air and were never at a loss for entertainment. If they weren't off on a walk with Kathleen looking for blueberries, they were inspecting the chickens or lying on their stomach watching the goldfish swim endlessly around the mosaic-bordered pool or talking to the pony, which they were allowed to ride with a groom walking beside them.

I doubt that Derek laid eyes on the little girls more than four or five times during our entire stay. Kathleen saw to that. They took their meals at a small table in the servants' dining room and used the back stairs to and from their bedroom, which was in a wing at the rear of the house. Fortunately the weather was exceptionally good that summer, and they were able to be outdoors most of the time. We had no prolonged periods of rain, only an occasional late-afternoon or evening thunder-shower, and that would be after Kathleen had brought them in to be bathed and fed.

While my mind was at rest about my younger sisters, it was anything but easy about Angie. She was too quiet and kept to herself so much that at times I wondered why she had begged me to visit her. I was puzzled, too, that she never left the estate, not even to go shopping. Didn't she want to? Or couldn't she for some reason?

I remember the morning I suggested a trip into town. I had caught the hem of my skirt on one of the rustic garden chairs and needed a spool of thread of a particular shade of green to mend it. "There must be a store in the village that would have it, Angie," I said. "Why don't we—"

"Oh no, Maudie," she interrupted. "There's no need for us to go. Just tell Mrs. Williams what you want, and when she goes in with James for supplies, she'll get it for you."

"But I'd like to go, Angie."

"No, we can't go," she said sharply. "Not now, anyway. I must see about the menus for lunch and dinner." With that, she left the terrace where we'd been sitting over a second cup of coffee and went quickly into the house, leaving me more puzzled than ever. It wasn't like her to be so short with me.

While it is true that we hadn't spent much time together since my arrival, she had been the soul of consideration, going out of her way to see to my comfort. She'd even had one of her dinner dresses altered to fit me and given me a necklace to wear with it.

I felt almost childishly disappointed at being denied a trip into town. Perhaps I was restless. In spite of all the wealth, the beauty of our surroundings, and the luxurious living quarters, I was not happy. I had too much time on my hands. Angie spent several hours a day alone in her room, and when I was left to my own devices, I filled the hours by taking lonely walks, arranging flowers in the cut-glass vases and silver bowls in the drawing room, or reading in Derek's library. More than once I found myself longing for the activity of the bookstore. At least I had that to look forward to in the fall. Mr. Heimlich had said he'd keep the position open for me. Since the summer months were so slow, he wouldn't need to hire anyone in my place.

When she *was* with me, Angie would try to give the impression that all was well with her world, but I could see that it was an effort. Each night as we sat around the candlelit dinner table, she played the part of the perfect hostess, smiling at Derek, encouraging me to join the conversation, but commenting only briefly herself. Whether she fooled Derek I cannot say, but it was obvious to me that she was merely acting the role expected of her, and I wondered how long she would keep it up. Angie had never been one to put up with things she didn't like, and it was clear to me that she was not content with life at Blauvelt House.

Derek, however, seemed quite satisfied. I remember one evening in particular when he looked happier than I had ever seen him as he talked about his last visit with the president in Washington, during the course of which he and Mr. Roosevelt had discovered that they had a common Dutch ancestor. "So you see, Angela," he said, leaning forward and smiling across the table at her, "the president and I are some kind of cousins—very distant, to be sure, but still cousins. I'm not sure how much that's going to weigh in my favor, but it can't hurt. In any case, he's asked me to work closely with the secretary of the treasury on some of the government's European investments."

"Who is the secretary of the treasury?" I was sure Angie asked the question only because she knew some show of interest was expected.

"George Cortelyou," Derek answered. "A good man, but I've heard it rumored that he's getting ready to step down. If he does, and if Roosevelt is reelected, I might just be in line for the appointment. Quite an honor, don't you think?"

He looked expectantly at Angie, his eyes sparkling as he waited for her approbation, and I suddenly understood why even the merest whisper of scandal that might be associated with his name had to be silenced. It was not, as Angie had thought, only his pride in the Blauvelt name (although that was certainly part of it) but also his desire for the honor and recognition he would gain should his "distant cousin" appoint him.

"Yes, Derek," Angie answered with a slight smile, the kind of smile one would bestow on a child who handed you his drawings to admire. "It would be quite an honor. Shall we have coffee in the drawing room?"

The day after I suggested a trip into town, my suspicions concerning Angie's state of mind were confirmed. Derek left for New York early in the morning, saying he would spend the night in the city and return the next afternoon. I saw Kathleen and the children off for the daily pony ride and went to look for Angie to see if she'd like fresh flowers in any of the rooms. I found her not in her bedroom, where I'd expected her to be, but in the gazebo at the far end of the garden, a small octagonal building with an ornamental cupola, furnished only with wooden benches under the seven rectangular openings that served as windows.

She was holding a full-blown blue hydrangea blossom (almost the deep, deep blue of her eyes) as she stared through the overhanging branches at the river, and she'd been crying. When she saw me, she dropped the flower and took a lace-edged handkerchief from her pocket. I waited, knowing it would do no good to ask what the trouble was. She'd tell me if and when she wanted me to know.

We sat in silence for a few moments. Then she blew her nose and looked me in the eye. "I don't know that I did you a favor bringing you here, Maudie. There's so little to amuse you—" She broke off and picked up the hydrangea again.

"Kitty and Megan are having the time of their lives," I said. "They're so much better off here than in the heat of the city. You know what it's like there in July and August."

"Yes, and I wish I were there right now," she cried. "Oh, Maudie, you have no idea what my life is like."

She pulled me closer to her and rested her head on my shoulder. I put my arm around her and waited. "I really don't know how much longer I can stand it," she said finally. "You've seen what it's like here. We see nobody, we go no place—oh, Maudie, I've been so lonesome! That's why I persuaded Derek to let you come. He won't invite anyone else, and he only allowed you to come because he thought you wouldn't know any of the people he knows."

"But why don't you go anyplace, Angie? Not even to the village?"

"Because I'm a prisoner here! I've been one ever since he came to Thirty-second Street for me that morning last winter! He's punishing me. If I went to the village, he'd know. Mrs. Williams would tell, or James—they're his spies. You see, he's given it out to New York society that I've been ill, but that's to keep me away from people until any talk there might have been dies down. I told you how he had me followed by a detective, remember? So I must live in seclusion. I can't stand it! I can't stand him—his lovemaking! At least I'll have my bed to myself tonight.''

I couldn't imagine James spying on anyone. Mrs. Williams, yes, but not that cheerful Irishman. I said nothing but sat thinking over what Angie had just told me until I saw her looking at me anxiously. "Why do you stay, Angie?" I asked. "A divorce—"

"He won't give me a divorce. No Blauvelt was ever divorced. They lived unhappily together for sixty or more years. . . . And besides, now he wants to be secretary of the treasury.''

"You could leave, Angie. Come and live with us.''

"On what? I tried that once. At least I thought about it the time I ran out of the house, but he came and made me go back. And if he let me stay with you, what would we do for money? But perhaps it would be worth it to be poor, just to be rid of him.''

Her expression changed suddenly as she glanced toward the house. "Look,'' she whispered. "There's Mrs. Williams now, checking up on me.''

I turned just in time to see the housekeeper's black-clad figure disappear behind the columns of the portico that fronted the house.

"She does that when Derek's away,'' Angie went on, "the nasty old snoop.''

When I asked how much longer she expected to be confined to the premises, Angie shrugged and said she had no idea, that Derek refused to say.

"If I were you—'' I began.

"I know, Maudie. You'd leave him and be penniless.''

"You could find work—"

"For eight dollars a week? How could I live on that? And I'd still be married to Derek."

"Surely he wouldn't let you starve. He'd settle something on you."

"You don't know Derek. He told me what he'd do. If I leave him, I'll be cut off without a cent, and he will no longer subsidize you three, because if he did, I might live off you. But as I said before, I couldn't live with you, anyway. He'd come and get me again, and persuade me to come back to him somehow or other. If I left here, I'd have to hide."

She sighed and stood up. "It's no good talking any more, Maudie. I'm caught, trapped, and I don't know how to free myself. Come on, it must be almost time for lunch."

She led the way out of the gazebo, carelessly stepping on the hydrangea blossom that had once again fallen to the floor.

X

The remainder of the summer seemed interminable. Left to myself, I would have made some excuse and gone home to New York and Mr. Heimlich, but that would have meant leaving Angie to a solitary life and depriving Kitty and Megan of a world they loved.

One consolation was Derek's library, a high-ceilinged room on the north side of the house that in spite of Mrs. Williams's thorough supervision of the housework, smelled slightly musty. I rather liked that, and I liked the special ladder that could be pushed along on a track to enable one to reach the higher shelves. Derek told me that he was not much of a reader—his father had amassed the superb collection of leather-bound classics—and that he seldom used the room. He preferred the study on the other side of the house, a smaller room next to the drawing room. I was welcome to spend as much time as I liked in the library, he said, as long as I returned the books to their proper places.

How Mr. Heimlich would have exclaimed over those tooled leather bindings! Dickens came in a warm Christmasy red,

Thackeray in green, and Sir Walter Scott in a blue the shade of one of his highland lakes. I read indiscriminately and for hours at a time. Whenever Angie indicated that she wanted to be alone, I'd curl up in one of the deep armchairs near the windows that overlooked the river and lose myself in the world of David Copperfield or Becky Sharp until I was wanted. I wasn't wanted very often. I don't know how Angie whiled away the hours, but I don't think she spent very many with Derek, at least during the day.

Nor do I know how Derek occupied himself. Occasionally I'd see him setting out on horseback, always with one of the grooms in attendance, and I knew he made regular inspection tours of the estate, but neither of these activities occupied more than a few morning hours. I seldom saw him between lunch and dinner. I think he must have spent the long summer afternoons in his study, the door to which was almost always closed.

In the evening he joined Angie and me in the drawing room for half an hour or so before going out to stroll up and down on the wide terrace while he smoked a cigar. I read, and Angie pretended to read, until Derek came back and said he thought he'd turn in, a signal for all of us to retire.

I could not help wondering whether he was as bored with life at Blauvelt House as Angie, and whether the trips to New York and Washington weren't a form of escape. Perhaps they were, but then, Derek was an astute businessman and not apt to neglect his responsibilities. He'd been kind to us too, and even if my summer was somewhat trying, he had provided Kitty and Megan with a far better one than I could have given them.

I remember only a single afternoon when things went wrong for them, and that was because they were frightened, not because they were unhappy or bored.

Shortly after lunch one day late in August, Kathleen came

to me saying that Cook had begged her to help the maids prepare the peaches for preserving. "So many ripened all at once, Miss Maud," she explained, "that they need me to peel them before they all go bad. T'would be a shame if they spoiled, it would."

"Of course, Kathleen," I said. "I'll take the children down to that clearing in the woods near the river. Maybe we'll find some blackberries."

"Oh, don't bring any home with you, Miss Maud! What with all them peaches, there's no room in the kitchen!"

I thought Kitty and Megan were somewhat subdued as we walked along the path next to the stone wall and into the nearby woods, and hoped they weren't coming down with something. Kathleen had told me that some of the help had been troubled with "summer complaint," a mild intestinal disorder. But by the time we reached the grassy knoll Megan called "the glad place" for some reason, they were their usual animated selves and set to work at once to mend a bird's nest they found on the ground.

I felt drowsy as I sat leaning against a tall maple, enjoying the warm sun on my face and arms, listening to the light voices of the children, and idly watching the boats on the river below. The sudden loud blast of the horn of a Hudson River Dayliner shattered the calm laziness of the afternoon, and when I saw clouds of black smoke pouring from its stacks, I could think of nothing but the smoke and flames of the *General Slocum*. I was unable to suppress an involuntary scream, and in a moment the two little girls were swarming over me wanting to know if I was hurt.

In the meantime the Dayliner sailed quietly on. The smoke disappeared, there were no further blasts of its horn, and my heart gradually stopped racing. But the children looked frightened.

"We thought the witch had hurt you," Kitty said, stroking my arm with her little brown hand.

"She said she would," Megan said.

"What on earth are you talking about?" I asked. "There are no witches——"

"That's what we call her."

"Call who?"

"Mrs. Williams," Megan said slowly. "She looks like a witch, and——"

"Let me tell!" Kitty cried. "We saw her. She was hurting Effie's arm. You know Effie, the maid? She was crying."

"Where did you see this?" I asked.

"This morning, when we were at the back door," Megan answered. "Kathleen told us to wait there for her. We could see into the kitchen. I guess Effie dropped something. There was broken glass on the floor, and Mrs. Williams said she'd have to give her money for it or she'd tell Uncle Derek."

"And then the witch saw us," Kitty broke in. "And she said if we told, she'd make you cry, Maudie, just as she made Effie cry. And so when you screamed, we thought she'd jumped out of the bushes——"

"Well, she didn't," I said brusquely. "And she wouldn't dare hurt me. The only reason I screamed was that I was startled by the boat's horn."

"It made me jump, too," Kitty said. "Will you tell us a story now, Maudie?"

Fortunately we returned to the city a few days after the witch episode, and although I was overjoyed to be back in New York, dusty streets and all, away from the brooding calm that hung over the house on the Hudson, I was not happy about leaving Angie. The expression on her face as she waved good-bye to us worried me; she was not tearful, nor did she look at all forlorn, which might have seemed natural under the circumstances. On the contrary, she looked almost happy, excited, as she stood on the steps of the portico with Derek's arm protectively around her waist. What bothered me most was the calculating look in her eyes, a look I had first seen when she was planning her campaign to ensnare a wealthy husband. The difference was that I *knew* what she was planning then . . .

We settled down to our old routine almost immediately. Kitty and Megan went back to school, Kathleen ran the house, and I returned to a warm welcome at the bookstore. Mr. Heimlich apologized for "letting things go a bit" when he saw me shake my head at the untidy accumulation of papers on his desk, and said he was beginning to have trouble finding things.

Danny gave me a hug and said that now maybe he could get on with the opus. He also said his studious friend, James Mahoney, would be glad to see me. "He must have asked me a dozen times when you'd be back, Maud. And once he quoted Tennyson to me—you know, 'Come into the garden, Maud.' Made a conquest there, by the looks of things," he said, grinning at me, then ambling off to his shelf.

Danny knew whereof he spoke. James Mahoney became quite attentive that fall, and I wasn't sure how to handle the situation. He was a personable young man, and I had nothing against him, but I was not ready for a serious attachment. I guess I mean that I wasn't in love with him, or with any of the others who took me out occasionally. At the time I didn't know what or who I was waiting for, but I did know it was not James Mahoney.

I wrote to Angie once a week, telling her about the bookstore, the children's progress in school, little things like that, but her replies were so general and noncommittal that I wondered if Derek (or Mrs. Williams) censored them. Later, much later, when I asked Derek if this was the case, he denied it, but that was several months after my sister disappeared.

XI

I was about to go up to bed the night Derek came to Thirty-second Street looking for Angie a second time. A cold November rain was beating against the parlor windows, and when the doorbell sounded at that late hour, I almost didn't answer it.

"I've come for Angela," he announced as soon as he had closed his umbrella and placed it in the stand in the corner of the vestibule. "Has she retired for the night?"

Without waiting for me to reply, he started for the stairs, but stopped abruptly when I said she wasn't in the house. He turned a shocked, angry face toward me, and when I saw the same peculiar brightness in his eyes that I had noticed the previous winter, I backed away from him.

"Not here?" he shouted. "Is that what you said? She must be here. Where else—you're not covering up for her, are you, Maud? Answer me!"

At first he wouldn't believe that I had not seen Angie since I returned to the city at the beginning of September or that I had not heard from her for the past two weeks. He kept insisting, sometimes almost incoherently, that she must be upstairs, and it was only when I offered to permit him to search the house that he came to his senses. At that point he sighed heavily and went slowly into the parlor where he sank down wearily onto the sofa.

"I don't know where she could have gone," he said in a normal tone as he rubbed his hand across his forehead. "She left Tarrytown sometime late last night or early this morning. I was on my way home from Washington, so I knew nothing about it until I arrived at Blauvelt House late this afternoon. The servants thought she was in her room, but when she neither rang for breakfast nor came down, they looked and found the room empty. After that, they searched the entire house. . . ."

"Could you tell what she took with her?" I asked.

"I didn't take time to look. My one thought was to follow her here. I had James drive me. I guess Mrs. Williams would know which clothes are missing. Angela had no money, as far as I know . . ."

"Well then, she couldn't go far, Derek. It wasn't raining earlier today. Maybe she went for a walk and fell, or turned her ankle—"

"My God!" he exclaimed, springing to his feet. "She could be lying helpless in the woods! And look at the weather now!"

I knew that it was extremely unlikely that Angie had gone for a walk in the woods (she used to say she despised all forms of exercise except dancing), but the thought gave Derek hope, and he phoned Blauvelt House at once, ordering a complete search of the grounds.

"Why did you keep her a prisoner, Derek?" I asked as soon as he returned to the parlor.

He looked startled for a moment, but then answered me calmly enough. "I simply wanted to protect her, to keep her safely away from malicious tongues. Angela was not always prudent, and after a particular incident occurred, I thought it best that she stay out of New York until it was forgotten. I tried to keep her happy, Maud. I gave her everything. You know that. She wanted for nothing. I was planning to take her to Europe again—oh, my God, I can't see why she'd go off—"

As if he suddenly realized he was shouting again, he broke off and covered his face with his hands. While I sat watching him, I could not help thinking how ridiculous he'd been to assume that keeping Angie isolated was a perfectly reasonable, even beneficial thing to do, but I did not want to argue the point with him just then. It was past eleven, and I was tired.

But Derek showed no sign of leaving until I asked him what further steps he intended to take.

"I don't know. I just don't know," he answered with a sigh as he stood up. "Not the police. I couldn't do that to Angela. Think of the publicity! It would ruin my chances in Washington! And aside from that, I couldn't do that to her—no, I couldn't! She's the whole world to me, Maud. I can't live without her. And I want her to be happy with me. I thought if we had a child it would help, but . . . Oh well, I'd better go. I'll be at the Fifth Avenue house tonight. If you hear from her, call me there at once. And tomorrow I'll probably go back to Tarrytown to see if I can find any trace of her."

I had trouble sleeping that night. Derek's outburst had shaken me, and try as I might, I could not reconcile the two sides of his character. The behavior of the angry, almost violent man who raged in the front hall was a far cry from that of the gentle, soft-spoken Derek I had come to know during the summer. He was the last person in the world I would have accused of instability, but who knows. . . .

A second cause of my wakefulness was that I half-expected Angie to come in quietly and slip into the bed next to mine. I knew she'd kept her key to the front door, possibly for just such an occasion. In the morning, however, there was no sign of her, and as I dressed, glancing from time to time at the empty bed, I realized how right I'd been about the excitement I'd seen in her face that last morning at Blauvelt House. She had begun, almost two months ago if not earlier, to plan another campaign, this time to escape from the man she had once set out to captivate.

During the next several weeks, Derek came to see me fairly frequently, either in the evening or on a Sunday afternoon, when he knew I'd be home. The initial shock of Angie's departure had worn off, and his emotions were under control, but I could tell she was seldom out of his thoughts. Perhaps he came because he felt closer to her in the Thirty-second Street house than in his own, or perhaps I was the only one to whom he could talk about her. He told me that as far as he could determine, she had taken nothing with her except some clothes and a few of the jewels he had given her.

"The detectives I hired were of the opinion that they might be able to trace her through the jewels if she tried to sell them," he said as we sat in the parlor having tea the Sunday before Christmas. "But so far, there's no sign of them. I've done everything I can think of, Maud, and now there's nothing to do but wait until she needs money. Then she'll have to come back to me. And when she does, things will be different."

"In what way will they be different?" I asked.

"In several ways. We'll travel, entertain—all that," he said, placing his teacup carefully on the piecrust table. "I made a mistake in keeping her at Blauvelt House. I knew—and I admit it freely now—that she was unhappy, but in spite of that I was convinced that I was doing the right thing, the only thing. I was trying to protect her."

"You've said that before, Derek," I said. "You should have

74

known that Angie wouldn't put up with that kind of treatment for very long. Are you sure you weren't protecting the Blauvelt name?''

He flushed angrily, and for a moment I thought he was going to storm out of the house. He stood up suddenly, but instead of leaving the room, he went over to the window where he remained for a few minutes with his back to me. When he turned around, the anger I had seen in his face had disappeared, replaced by an expression of puzzled thoughtfulness.

''Oh yes, of course that came into it,'' he said quietly. ''But I'm beyond all that now. The Washington appointment is off since Roosevelt lost to Taft in the election. I shouldn't have let it matter so much to me. Believe me, Maud, I just want Angela back. I'll do whatever she wants. . . .''

I pitied him at that point, but I was afraid anything I said might make him feel more abject than he already did. Fortunately, just as the silence between us was beginning to pall, Kitty and Megan came clattering down the stairs and paused for a moment at the parlor door. For some reason, they both waved and smiled at Derek, something they'd never done before, and then hurried down the hall to the kitchen. He prepared to leave soon after that, and as I saw him to the door, he took some bills from his wallet and asked me to buy a few extra Christmas presents ''for the little girls.''

''Come and have Christmas dinner with us, Derek,'' I said impulsively. ''That is, if you're not busy.''

''Thank you, Maud. I'd like that,'' he said with the barest hint of a smile before turning away and going out into the light snow that had been falling all afternoon.

With the money Derek gave me I bought a doll's house, complete with miniature furnishings. I remembered how I had longed for one, and how years ago I had envied Maria Bishoff the one her father made for her. Since we were all too busy at the bookstore to take time off and since my lunch hour wasn't long enough for me to go all the way across town to Le Marque's Toy Store on Broadway, I had to do my shopping at night.

It was dark, windy, and cold when I was hurrying home carrying my bulky purchase, or I might have taken more notice of the other shoppers. Had I been more alert, I might have known for certain whether the tall, slender woman who passed me with her head bent against the wind was Angie. It wasn't the first time I'd caught a glimpse of someone who reminded me of her. One day I even followed a woman for half a block before seeing that she was a stranger. I hurriedly shifted my package to my other hand and turned around for a second look, but by that time she had disappeared into the crowd of people at the crossing.

After a moment's hesitation I went on home, and with Kathleen's help hid the doll's house behind some cartons in the storeroom. I decided against mentioning the episode to Derek; it wouldn't do any good, I thought, and might just make him more unhappy than he already was.

On Christmas Day he arrived shortly before dinner, laden with presents for everyone: a big doll for each of the children, a fur muff for me, and a pair of fur-lined gloves for Kathleen. Kitty and Megan dragged him over to see the doll's house, and I could tell he was gratified by their delight in it. He was made to squat down on the floor while they explained its tiny wonders to him—the little doors that opened and closed, the rocking chair that really rocked, and so on.

He seemed a different man—a happy man—as he agreed that a chair should be moved here or a table there, and I wondered why on earth we had kept the children out of his way during the summer at Blauvelt House. Was it Angie's idea? Or Mrs. Williams's orders? As I watched the three of them that Christmas afternoon, I noticed that he kept glancing at Megan. It occurred to me that he might have noticed her resemblance to Angie for the first time and felt drawn to her.

If he was startled when Kathleen sat down at the table with us, he didn't show it. He was, as I should have known, the perfect guest, carving the turkey for us, praising the flavor of the gravy, and patiently answering the children's questions about the welfare of the pony, the chickens, and the other animals at the house on the Hudson. The dinner, so different from the quiet formal meals I had had with him and Angie during the summer, was in its own way a tremendous success, and we all knew it.

Later, when Derek and I were sitting in front of the parlor fire, he told me it was necessary for him to go to London and Paris right after the first of the year.

"As you can imagine, I hate to leave right now, Maud, for fear—"

"Yes, I know," I said, "but couldn't I ask your office to cable you if—"

"Of course. Here's the telephone number. Ask for Mr. Blanchard. He'll know where to reach me. I wish I could put this trip off, but there are matters in both cities that need my attention." He was silent for a moment or two and then surprised me by asking me to tell him a little about the bookstore. I think he may have done that to steer the conversation away from anything concerning Angie, but maybe not. He did seem interested in what I had to say.

He didn't stay late but took his leave about half past eight after promising to bring Kitty and Megan some inhabitants for the doll's house the next time he came.

"You need some people to live in your house," he said seriously. "A mother, a father—"

"And children," Megan suggested.

"And a cook!" Kitty shouted. "They must have things to eat."

"Of course they must," Derek agreed with a smile. "And indeed they shall have a cook, a fine one. And now I must be on my way. Thank you, Maud, for the evening, quite the nicest one I've had in a long while. I'll be in touch with you before I sail."

XII

When there was no word from or about Angie by the end of January, I gave up hope of ever seeing her again, and I think Derek may have done so as well. He returned from Europe early in February, and except to tell me that he had dismissed the detectives (who had had no success in their search for her and were inclined to think she had left the city), he did not refer to her during his visits to Thirty-second Street. I knew he couldn't have put her out of his mind altogether, though, and I had to admire the way he carried on with his life, so different from the way my father had reacted to Mama's disappearance into the East River.

To the delight of Kitty and Megan, he seldom came empty-handed, and when I reproached him one evening for spoiling us as well as supporting us, he looked surprised.

"But you're my family, aren't you?" he asked. "My sisters-in-law?"

I could see that he felt some responsibility for us, but I could not see why he should. After all, he was the injured party. Angie had hurt him badly, tricking him into marrying her and then leaving him. A less compassionate man would have turned his back on us. Perhaps, however, he looked upon us as a worthy charity case.

The spring of that year, 1909, was uneventful, except that shortly before my twentieth birthday in April I had two proposals of marriage, both of which I refused. One was from James Mahoney, the other from a middle-aged widower who patronized the bookstore. James was hurt, I know (Danny said the right word was *crestfallen*), but the widower merely shrugged his shoulders and took his trade elsewhere.

Mr. Heimlich laughed and said not to worry about losing him as a customer since he seldom bought a book anyway.

"But you will go off one of these days, Maud," he said, "leaving me in the lurch again."

I had no intention of leaving him permanently, but when Derek suggested that we spend a second summer in Tarrytown with him, I hesitated to ask for the time off. I was not particularly anxious to return to the place where Angie had been so miserable, but I didn't want to offend the man who had been so kind to us. Besides, Kitty and Megan (and even Kathleen) were excited at the prospect of a summer in the country. I was the only one among us who had any reservations.

Derek, noticing my hesitation, was quick to reassure me.

"I can understand why you might have some doubts concerning the wisdom of returning there, Maud," he said when we were alone, "but don't worry. It won't be at all like last year. Things will be different. Mrs. Williams is no longer there, and you and the little girls will have the run of the place, without her hovering around." He paused for a moment, then smiled at me. "And if Mr. Heimlich doesn't give you your job back in the fall, I'll buy you a bookstore for yourself."

Mr. Heimlich was not at all upset when I told him I would be away for July and August. He said he had no objection but that Danny would be hard to get along with for those months, just as he was last year.

"But you go ahead, Maud. I'll just have to ignore his grumpiness," he went on, patting Danny on the shoulder. "I'll give him an extra half hour for lunch, so he can get on with his masterpiece. Summer's a slow time, anyway."

That spring had been a busy one for all three of us. We'd had difficulty keeping up with the demand for some of the more popular novels of the year, particularly John Fox, Jr.'s *Trail of the Lonesome Pine* and Mrs. Rinehart's detective story, *The Man in Lower Ten*. It had been a profitable season too, and Mr. Heimlich raised my salary to ten dollars a week, which I continued to secrete in the shoe box—I can't imagine why.

The atmosphere at Blauvelt House the summer of 1909 was decidedly lighter without the presence of Mrs. Williams. I think even Derek was relieved that she had left to take care of an invalid sister. She had been replaced by a Mrs. Van Tieck, a cheerful Dutch woman who welcomed Kitty and Megan as if they were her own grandchildren. James was instructed to drive us wherever we wanted to go, and Derek organized outings and picnics, even a ferryboat ride over to Nyack. (I went on that trip reluctantly; the memory of the *General Slocum* was still all too vivid.)

The informality of our lives delighted me. The children no longer had to go to the meadow to romp. They had the freedom of the house and grounds and could make as much noise as they chose. They took their meals with us in the dining room, with the result that our dinners were considerably more lively than the ones I had endured the previous summer.

Contrary to my expectations, I was not haunted by thoughts of Angie. I did not keep expecting to see her coming down the wide staircase dressed in something flowing and graceful or idling on the terrace over a cup of tea. I did, however, feel a slight pang when I looked out my window one afternoon and saw Kitty and Megan "playing house" in the gazebo where the blue hydrangeas were in full bloom. One morning when the master bedroom was being cleaned, I had a glimpse of some of her dresses hanging in the closet, but other than that I could see no sign that Angie had ever lived in Blauvelt House. When Megan asked for her one night at dinner, Derek said she was away visiting friends, which seemed to satisfy her because she began at once to prattle away about the new pony cart and how the groom allowed her to hold the reins. As far as I can remember, neither she nor Kitty asked for her again, which wasn't really surprising; after all, they'd seen very little of her since her marriage.

Derek went to New York several times a week, occasionally staying overnight at his club since the Fifth Avenue house was closed for the summer, but sometimes returning the same day. I was always glad to see him arrive in the late afternoon, for while I was certainly not alone in the mansion at night, I could not overcome a slight but definite feeling of uneasiness when he wasn't there.

I tried to tell myself that any nervousness or apprehension on my part was foolish, that in addition to the housekeeper and Kathleen, two maids and a cook were living under the same roof with me, within call. On the other hand, the servants' wing, with its own staircase and facilities, was a fair distance from the large formal rooms in the front part of the house. I felt very much alone when I sat reading in the drawing room or in the library after Kitty and Megan were in bed.

All houses, large or small, have their idiosyncracies, their rattles and creaks, which after one has identified them present no problem. I had not lived in Blauvelt House long enough, however, for its various sounds to become familiar to me and would find myself looking over my shoulder when a board settled or a curtain rustled. In the end, I gave up trying to overcome my fears, and when Derek wasn't there, I simply took my book into my own room after I'd said good night to the children. There I could read in comfort until I felt sleepy.

The evenings Derek spent at home were full of activity. After dinner we'd play Parcheesi, or weather permitting, croquet with Kitty and Megan. Later on, he and I might stroll along the path that bordered the property at the edge of the river. Sometimes on those walks he'd talk about Angie and how he missed her.

"She owns me, body and soul, Maud," he said more than once. "Without her I feel as if I'm only half alive."

I knew, somehow, that he didn't expect me to say anything, just to listen to the yearnings he kept hidden from the rest of the world.

"I'd do anything to have her back with me," he went on. "Anything. I don't dare let myself think what I might do if I found her with another man. Oh, don't look frightened, Maud! I assure you that my emotions are completely under control. And you and the girls help me take my mind off her."

That was an unusual outburst for Derek; most of our evenings together were given to lighter conversation or occasionally a game of cribbage, and they were on the whole quite pleasant. Perhaps that's why I found the evenings without him trying—that's all they were, merely trying—until the rainy night at the beginning of August when someone broke into the house.

I had heard nothing but loud claps of thunder and heavy rain during the night. The next morning, as soon as I discovered what had happened, I left a message for Derek at his office saying there'd been a robbery, and then phoned the local police. The detective, who came within minutes, a Lieutenant Ruysman, said that whoever had smashed the pane of glass in one of the French doors of the study must have timed his blow to coincide with a thunderclap. Otherwise one of us would have heard the crash of broken glass.

"And once he had knocked out the glass, all he had to do was reach in and turn the handle. That kind of lock is no deterrent to a sneak thief," he said, stepping carefully around the shards on the floor.

"I wonder if he knew the master was not at home," Mrs. Van Tieck said, glancing at the gaping drawers of the desk and the papers scattered over the carpet. "Did he get into the safe, do you think?"

"He knew where it was, all right," the detective answered, pointing to a painting, a scene of the Hudson above West Point, that had been tossed carelessly on the leather couch. "He knew just which picture covered the door to the safe. If he'd taken down any of the other paintings, chances are they'd be crooked, or off center, or even on the floor, but they've not been disturbed."

"But did he open it?" Mrs. Van Tieck persisted.

"I can't be sure, ma'am, but I doubt it. We'll have to wait for Mr. Blauvelt—I understand he's on his way—to come and see if anything's missing. Has anything been taken from the room? Can you tell?"

Since none of us knew what Derek kept in his desk, we couldn't say whether anything was missing there, but the rest of the furnishings appeared to be intact. His collection of antique jade in its glass case was untouched, and the ancient Chinese vase, which he would allow no one but himself to dust, was in its place at one end of the mantelpiece, while at the opposite end an old carriage clock ticked quietly.

When he received no answer, the detective sighed and said

there was nothing more to be done until Mr. Blauvelt returned.

Derek arrived in a hired car shortly before noon, and to my surprise his first concern was for us, not for any theft or damage to his possessions.

"Are you all right, Maud?" he asked as he hurried up the shallow steps of the portico. "The children? They weren't hurt?"

I assured him that we were all unharmed and that Kitty and Megan knew nothing about the break-in. "I told Kathleen to keep them busy in the kitchen until it was time for them to go down to the stables," I said. "Lieutenant Ruysman is waiting for you in the study."

I was reading, or rather, trying to read in the cool comfort of the library when Derek came looking for me.

"Nothing was taken, Maud," he said, sinking into one of the large armchairs. "We think that when he couldn't open the safe, he went on a rampage through my desk, looking for the key and a memorandum of the combination. You need both to open it.

"Actually, there's not very much in that safe, just a couple of thousand in cash, some jewels of Angela's—the family jewels are in the bank vault—and a copy of my will."

"Have you any idea who it might have been?" I asked.

"Someone who knew the place, undoubtedly. I've had various workmen here from time to time—repairing the roof, clearing out the gutters, that sort of thing. And this past spring I had that terrace outside the study rebuilt with flagstones because the old slates that had been there for years were beginning to chip. Oh, I don't know, Maud—I wouldn't have any idea which one to suspect."

"Mrs. Van Tieck wondered if it might have been someone who knew you were away last night."

"Well, I won't be away at night again. If the office needs me, I'll go down and come back the same day. In the meantime I'll see about having special locks put on all the first-floor doors and windows. I wouldn't want to have them barred. That would spoil the facade of the house."

I do not remember the rest of the conversation, but I do remember wondering if Derek suspected that the culprit was Angie, come back for her jewels. If he did think so, he never admitted it, and although the thought that it could have been she crossed my mind several times in the next few days, I couldn't bring myself to voice it.

Neither could I bring myself to ask Derek about the unexpected reappearance of Mrs. Williams a few days later. I had just come in from the garden and was crossing the wide front hall with a vase of roses in my hands when she drove up in a taxi. She ignored me, brushed past the parlormaid, and knocked sharply on the door of the study.

I thought that if Derek rehired her as housekeeper, I would make some excuse to leave at once, even at the risk of hurting him. Kitty and Megan were terrified of her, and I had distrusted her from the beginning. She didn't stay long, however. Her business with Derek must have been settled quickly. Not more than half an hour had elapsed when I saw her drive off in another taxi. Evidently Derek had telephoned for it.

I sighed with relief and waited for an explanation from him, but he never mentioned the incident.

As the last lovely days of August slipped by and we could feel the first hints of fall in the air, I began to look forward to our return to the city. I wasn't as anxious to get back as I'd been the previous summer, but two months of idleness, however pleasurable, was long enough. Kitty and Megan, on the other hand, were so reluctant to leave Blauvelt House that Derek said he'd see if we could all spend the long Thanksgiving weekend there. Kitty wanted to know how far away that was, and Megan said she'd come only if he promised that we wouldn't eat the big turkey they had named Jumbo.

"He knows his name," she said, "and comes to the fence when we call him."

Derek assured her we'd have a completely strange bird for our dinner and saw us off, laden with hampers of fresh fruit and vegetables Mrs. Van Tieck had packed for us.

We arrived home in the middle of the afternoon, and hadn't been in the house more than half an hour when Kathleen, who had gone straight to the kitchen to put away the produce, came hurrying into the parlor where I was raising the shades that had been lowered all summer. "Miss Maud, Miss Maud!" she called breathlessly. "I think, I mean I can see—" She broke off and turned to glance quickly around the room, as if checking its contents.

"What is it, Kathleen?"

"It's my pots and pans, miss. They've been moved. I can tell. Someone's been here."

I didn't doubt her for a minute. She had a special place for each cooking utensil—cake pans here, soup kettles there, and roasting pans down below. Kitty and Megan used to tease her by chanting "a place for everything and everything in its place" when they were allowed to help in the kitchen.

"And I never in the world would have left crumbs in the breadbox, Miss Maud. We'll have mice, for sure."

"We left in a hurry that morning, Kathleen. Do you suppose—"

"No, Miss Maud, I didn't forget. The last thing I did was to throw out a few crusts of bread for the birds and wipe the box with a damp cloth. Oh, I can't abide the thought of mice, Miss Maud."

The cupboards were disarranged, but only slightly, and I

don't think I would have noticed that anything was out of place if it hadn't been called to my attention. I couldn't argue with Kathleen, though. The pots didn't rearrange themselves, and there *were* crumbs in the breadbox.

"We should have a cat, miss," she said. "The girls would love it, and we could shut it up in here at night. That's when the mice come out, the nasty things."

The thought that she was more afraid of mice in the house than of an intruder made me smile, but I wasn't smiling later on when I discovered that my shoe box was empty. I think I knew then that Angie had been living in the house for at least part of the time we were away and that she had helped herself to my savings, just as she had once helped herself to the money in Papa's bureau drawer.

The next morning, however, I wasn't so sure it had been Angie, and I was glad I had resisted the impulse to telephone Derek the previous evening and perhaps raise his hopes unnecessarily. After breakfast, and after Kathleen left to take the children to school, saying she'd do some marketing on the way back, I went upstairs to search for some trace of Angie's presence. I wasn't sure what I was looking for—a hairpin, perhaps, something small that she might have overlooked when she left.

I found nothing in any of the bedrooms that might even hint that she had been there, but in the bathroom, on the floor behind the wicker laundry hamper, lay a pair of dark socks, a man's socks. They were dirty, and one of them had a hole in the toe. I picked them up gingerly and was still holding them when Kathleen called me to come down and see the kitten she had bought from the grocer for ten cents.

XIII

I realized almost immediately that there were two possibilities to be considered: Either some unknown male had been living in the house doing his own cooking, or Angie had brought a companion with her. I thought the latter the more probable. She was the one who had a key, and I could see no sign of forced entry, no broken locks or windows. I thought of asking the neighbors if they had seen anyone coming or going while we were away but then decided against it. I didn't know them well at all, just to nod and say good morning to in the street. Besides, the ones who lived on either side of us went away for the entire summer every year.

I said nothing to anyone about the missing money—or the socks, which I wrapped in tissue paper and put in the shoe box. It seemed a proper place for them, somehow. If Angie ever came back looking for more cash, she'd get a surprise, or if Mr. X had been living alone in our house, and came back looking for money, he'd be surprised to find his socks instead. And my salary would be in the savings bank on the corner.

Strangely enough, I was more puzzled than frightened, at

least at that point. If I had been afraid, I suppose I would have told Derek or notified the police. No, I wasn't frightened then, but over the Thanksgiving weekend all that changed. Derek was disappointed that I couldn't go up to Tarrytown with him and the children for the holiday, but I had been home with a heavy cold accompanied by a persistent cough, and since Dr. Sullivan had advised me to stay indoors, I didn't feel I should make the trip.

Kathleen left soups and stews in the icebox for me, things I could easily heat up, and the three of them drove off with Derek right after school on Wednesday afternoon. The empty house seemed remarkably peaceful without them, and after an early supper I went up to bed and slept soundly for almost ten hours.

Thanksgiving, a cold and cloudy day, dragged miserably. I felt too listless to settle down to any little household chores or even to one of the novels Mr. Heimlich had lent me, and by four o'clock in the afternoon when I sat by the fire sipping a cup of tea, I was longing for the sound of a human voice. Goldilocks, the kitten (named for her tawny coloring), lay dozing on the hearthrug, and after watching her for a while, I felt my own eyes drooping.

I must have fallen asleep, for the ringing of the telephone in the front hall startled me so that I nearly upset the teapot when I struggled up to answer it. It stopped ringing before I could pick up the receiver. A wrong number, I thought, and after waiting a moment to see if it would ring again, I washed up the tea things and fed the cat. Without bothering about an evening meal, I went upstairs and got into bed after taking two teaspoonfuls of the elixir Dr. Sullivan had left. He said it would suppress my cough and let me sleep.

When I woke, it was still dark. I lay quietly, thinking that I'd made a mistake in going to bed so early and wondering what time it was. I heard a dog bark somewhere in the neighborhood, and after that it was a night as quiet as the ones I had known in Tarrytown. If it had been stormy, with the wind and rain rattling the windows, I probably never would have known anyone was on the stairs, but as it was, the distinctive creak of one of the steps, the fourth from the top, alerted me.

I sat up in bed, more terrified than I'd been since I felt myself falling from the deck of the *General Slocum* into the East River.

I wanted to be absolutely silent and listen, but at that moment I was seized with a paroxysm of coughing. By the time it subsided and I could hear again, all was quiet. I lay back in bed, exhausted but unable to sleep, and after a while I got up and lighted the gas fixture on the wall near the door. Somehow that was comforting, and I lay watching it flicker until I could see a faint streak of daylight in the eastern sky.

I went slowly down the stairs, testing the fourth one from the top, which creaked even under my weight. I could find no sign that anything had been disturbed, and nothing seemed to be missing. By the time I finished my breakfast, the sun was pouring in through the east windows, and everything looked so familiar, so normal, that I began to wonder if I had imagined the noise in the night. But I knew I hadn't. I knew what I'd heard, and the stair never creaked by itself. I also knew that it couldn't have been Angie, who let herself in with her key. She would have remembered the fourth step from the top. It had to have been someone else, using her key, with or without her knowledge.

As soon as I was dressed, I went out, cough or no cough, to find a locksmith.

Friday passed without incident. Once the locks were changed on the front and back doors and chains installed for added protection, I was able to relax. I couldn't help feeling a bit guilty, though, as if I were being disloyal to my sister. Suppose she was in desperate straits and needed shelter, only to find her key didn't work? But surely we'd hear her if she knocked. . . .

On Saturday morning I felt so much better that I spent the day at the bookstore catching up on the typing that had accumulated while I was home Wednesday and Friday. Kind Mr. Heimlich asked me at least once an hour if I was sure I felt up to the work, and Danny gave me a small box of lemon drops, which, he said, were the next best thing to hot lemon and honey for a cold.

It was dusk when I rounded the corner of Lexington Avenue and Thirty-second Street on my way home, and as I approached the house, hurrying because of the cold wind, I saw a dark-clad figure cross the street and stand at the bottom of our stoop.

"Angie?" I cried as soon as I was close enough to see that it was a woman. "Angie! Where have you—"

I stopped abruptly, puzzled that she didn't answer me and by the fact that she was wearing a heavy veil that concealed her face. A moment later, I felt strong fingers take hold of my arm and heard a vaguely familiar voice say:

"No, I am not your sister. I have come to fetch her. You had better take me inside."

With this, she propelled me up the steps and indicated that I should unlock the door. I had no choice but to do as she said. I tried to shake her off, pull away from her, but her grip was like iron. Once inside, she let go of me so that I could light the gas fixture in the hall. When I turned to look at her, she lifted the veil—it was like the ones widows wear in mourning—and I found myself staring into the small mean eyes of the former housekeeper at Blauvelt House.

XIV

"I said I have come to fetch Angie," Mrs. Williams repeated, sounding as if she had just stopped in to borrow a book.

"She isn't here," I said, "and I have no idea of her where-abouts. Now, will you be good enough to leave my house?"

I spoke as calmly as I could, but I had to hold my hands clasped together to keep them from shaking. She did not reply, but turned abruptly and strode into the parlor, ordering me to light the lamps as she went. I did so, but only because I wanted to be able to see her.

"I have it on good authority that she has been seen here," she said, settling herself on the sofa as if she meant to stay. "And I am prepared to wait until you produce her, or tell me where she is hiding."

Some people, and I've met two or three of them during my life, have the ability to instill fear in others merely by their presence, and Mrs. Williams was one of them. She had been responsible for the subdued atmosphere at Blauvelt House, not Derek. I had seen the help cringe at her approach, and as she sat in the parlor staring at me, I was reminded of poor little

Effie, the maid who dropped a glass and looked frightened to death every time the housekeeper spoke to her—the maid the children had seen crying—and I had to use all my self-control to conceal my own fright. I said nothing, afraid I might stammer or stutter.

I don't know how long we sat in silence—perhaps five minutes, perhaps longer. I thought from the way she cocked her head from time to time she was listening for any sound that would indicate the presence of another person in the house, but maybe she was waiting for me to break down under her concentrated stare and confess that I knew where my sister was. I half-expected her to make a thorough search of the house, but she never moved from the sofa. She just listened.

At last she stood up and fastened her cloak.

"Be assured that I shall find her," she said, looking down at me. "Angela is in my debt, and I am not one to let such things go."

Turning quickly, she glided into the hall and let herself out. As soon as I heard the door close behind her, I made sure it was locked and that the chain was in position.

Angie must have borrowed the money from Mrs. Williams before she disappeared from Blauvelt House, I thought as I heated up a pot of lamb stew for my dinner. It didn't seem likely to me that the housekeeper would have a vast sum available, but neither was it likely that she would make such a fuss about a few dollars. None of it made any sense, but that didn't stop me from worrying about strong measures Mrs. Williams might adopt. The cruel grip she had had on my arm was evidence enough of her sadistic nature, and I could easily imagine how promptly she would mete out severe punishment to any who crossed her. If only Angie would settle up with her . . .

I wondered, as I prepared for bed that night, if it could have been Mrs. Williams who lived in our house during the summer, the one who helped herself to my savings, and then decided it couldn't have been she. She might have misplaced the pots and pans, but she would never have left a pair of dirty socks behind the hamper.

The entire situation was becoming too unpleasant, too complicated for me, and before going to sleep, I decided to set it all before Derek as soon as he returned the next day.

"You look as if you have something on your mind, Maud," he said when he had ushered his three charges into the house late Sunday afternoon. "What is it? Is your cold worse?"

When I assured him that I felt much better but would like to talk to him privately, he said he thought it would do me good to get out and invited me to have dinner with him in a French restaurant he knew. At the moment I couldn't think of anything I would rather do and accepted with alacrity.

"They concentrate on the food here, Maud," he said when we were seated at a table covered with a plain white cloth and lighted by a candle in a small pewter holder. "No elaborate decorations, just splendid food."

The meal was superb, beginning with a hearty onion soup, followed by chicken in a light wine sauce, and ending with a delicious lemon soufflé. I was enjoying it so much that I waited until we were having coffee before launching into an account of the recent troubling events.

He listened intently while I told him about the pots and pans and the bread crumbs. I remember that he was still smiling slightly at Kathleen's fear of mice and her immediate purchase of a kitten when I mentioned finding the socks. Then three things happened almost simultaneously: All color drained away from Derek's face; he started so violently that he upset the remains of his coffee; and a waiter came running. Neither of us spoke, and by the time the table had been tidied, Derek had regained his composure and asked me to continue.

When I finished my account, he took a pen and a small notebook from his pocket.

"Let's see what we have," he said, turning to a blank page, and speaking as he wrote:

1. *Angela, according to Mrs. Williams, is in the city. That means she's been able to stay well hidden, or the detectives would have found her.*

2. *One way or another she is indebted to Mrs. Williams.*

3. *Mrs. Williams is determined to find her.*

4. *Angela may or may not have spent the summer, or part of it, in your house.*

5. *The owner of the socks was in the house, either on his own or with Angela.*

At this point Derek stopped writing and stared down at the page. "Or with Angela," he said slowly, and I noticed a muscle at the corner of his mouth begin to twitch. "Well, let's get on with it."

6. *Either Angela or the unknown man took your savings.*

7. *The unknown man was probably the one you heard on the stairs. As you said, Angela would have known about the creak in the fourth one from the top.*

He paused and looked at me thoughtfully. "Anything else?" he asked.

"Do you think, Derek, that whoever phoned me on Thanksgiving Day did it to see if anyone was home? Remember, I'd been asleep, and the ringing may have gone on long enough so that he assumed the house was empty. And another thing: Could the person on the stairs have told Mrs. Williams he heard someone cough, and she thought it might be Angie? She knew, somehow, that Angie had been seen in this neighborhood.''

''Yes, to your first question, Maud, but I doubt that your night visitor would have been in touch with Mrs. Williams. It is likely that he is close to Angela, in which case he could have led Mrs. Williams directly to her, and she would have had no need to come to you for information about her.''

''I don't like Mrs. Williams, Derek; I'm afraid——''

''You needn't be concerned about her bothering you again. I'll see that she keeps away from you. I know how to reach her through her sister, the one she left my employ to nurse. I must say I was glad to be rid of her. I only kept her on because she'd been housekeeper for my parents, and my mother set great store by her. She's a strange, secretive woman, Maud, and I don't like her any more than you do.''

I was about to ask him what she'd wanted when she arrived at Blauvelt House last summer, but just then the waiter came with the bill, and it slipped my mind.

I had thought Derek would be glad to know that Angie was probably in the city and excited at the prospect of finding her, but the restrained way he referred to her surprised me.

''Aren't you anxious to find Angie, Derek? Won't you hire the detective agency again, now——''

''Of course I'm anxious, Maud,'' he said quietly. ''It's just that I don't want to get my hopes up, and then . . .''

The cab stopped at our door at that point, and after Derek had seen me safely inside, he took his leave without saying anything further about his wife.

I did not hear from him again for almost a week. He came the next Saturday evening after the children were in bed, and

I sensed at once from his manner that he'd reached a decision or at least determined on a course of action.

"I don't know whether you've guessed it or not, Maud," he said when we were seated in the parlor, "but my feelings for Angela have undergone a change, quite a change."

He paused when Kathleen came in with a tray.

"Ah, Kathleen, you've remembered my favorite biscuits," he said with a smile as I poured the cocoa she had made. He waited until she had gone, then sat back and looked at me thoughtfully before he spoke. "You see, I knew from the beginning that she didn't love me, but it didn't matter. I was infatuated with her beauty, half mad with desire, and I knew she wanted wealth—she admitted that openly. I thought that my money and what it could do would keep her happy, or at least content, with me. But it wasn't enough. I was too old for her, too stodgy. Then, through the entrée I gave her into society she met a number of handsome young men—I know I am not much on looks—and delighted in their company. After a while there was an affair, the knowledge of which almost destroyed me. If she came back to me now, I'm afraid things wouldn't be any different, and to tell the truth, I couldn't go through that again. I don't believe she'd come back in any case, and I keep telling myself I'm better off without her. . . ."

He stared at the fire for a moment or two, then sat up straight, removed a check book from an inner pocket, and placed it on the table in front of him.

"Now, what to do. First, Mrs. Williams. Obviously Angela borrowed money from her—I don't think she'd steal—and hasn't repaid it, but I do not believe Mrs. Williams will trouble you again. If by any chance she does, write her a check for whatever she demands, up to a thousand dollars. I have opened a special account in your name, Maud, and deposited ten thousand in it."

"But what are the rest of the checks for, Derek? I'd just need one."

"You may need more, Maud. It is necessary for me to go abroad again, and I don't know how long I'll be away this time or I wouldn't burden you with this. Secondly, we come to Angela. She is still my wife, and in spite of her behavior I cannot allow her to be in want, as she may very well be. There is a good chance she'll appeal to you for funds, and I leave it to you to decide how much to give her. I wouldn't, however, write a check for more than a hundred dollars at one time. She's apt to be careless about money.

"One more thing. I dislike the thought of your being worried that someone might break in. I don't think Angela would know how, but one of her lovers might, and frighten you and the little girls. James will be at the Fifth Avenue house while I am away, acting as caretaker—I've given the rest of the staff some time off—and I suggest that you telephone him any time you feel nervous. He could be here in twenty minutes. I will instruct him to lose no time in responding to your call.

"Now, let me see. Is there something else?" He frowned as he consulted his notebook again, and then looked at me inquiringly.

"I can't think of anything else, Derek. You're doing so much for us, and I don't know how to thank you."

"But I'm leaving you to deal with my wife. It's not fair of me, Maud, but it's better that I don't see her, or have any contact with her. We'd both be miserable. I owe you a vote of thanks, my dear sister-in-law. You and the children pulled me out of the doldrums. Don't think I'm not grateful."

He left a few minutes later, saying he'd be in touch with me as soon as he returned from Europe, whenever that might be. I washed the cocoa cups, thinking he'd chosen a strange way of dealing with Angie, but I supposed it was the only choice a man like Derek could make—one that not only permitted him the satisfaction of having done his duty but also prevented any unpleasantness. Somewhat like avoiding the "occasion of sin," as we'd been warned to do in Sunday school.

I went upstairs slowly, thinking over what Derek had said during his visit, and my heart ached for him when I remembered the longing—or was it the pain?—I had seen in his eyes when he spoke of Angie. I also remembered how upset he'd been in the restaurant when he realized that Angie might well have spent the summer in our house with another man. In spite of all he'd said about not being able to live with her, I knew he'd take her back in a minute, and on almost any terms.

XV

As they so often do, the weeks between Thanksgiving and Christmas went by in a flash. The bookstore did a thriving business, with orders for Dr. Eliot's *Five Foot Shelf* accounting for a good share of the profits. We were so rushed that instead of going home for lunch I took a sandwich with me and ate it at my desk. Danny complained that it would take him all of January to get back into the "writing mood," while Mr. Heimlich bounced around, beaming at the customers and getting in everyone's way.

Beautifully wrapped boxes arrived from Derek (he must have ordered them before he left for Europe) a few days before Christmas, causing excited speculation about their contents. I did my own shopping one clear, cold evening, and as I was carrying my packages home, I was reminded of the tall, slender woman I had seen the year before, the night I bought the doll's house.

Angie had been gone for more than a year by that time. Since I'd heard nothing further from Mrs. Williams and no one else had attempted to intrude on us, I assumed that my sister had found some source of income and settled up with the housekeeper. I knew Derek would be curious, but when I wrote to tell him I hadn't had to use any of the checks he left, I did so without mentioning Angie, since he'd made no reference to her in the one letter I'd received from him.

All in all, it was a good Christmas, but I couldn't help feeling a bit envious when a starry-eyed Kathleen showed me the diamond ring Patrick Houlihan, her redheaded suitor, gave her on Christmas Eve. She must have thought I was concerned about losing her because she was quick to say that they wouldn't be able to afford to marry for another year.

"And even then, Miss Maud, I could come in days if you'd like," she said, holding the ring up to the light and admiring its sparkle. "If Pat hadn't spent so much on this diamond, we might have married sooner, but what can you do with a stubborn Irishman when he's made up his mind to do something?"

Nothing, I thought, remembering my father and hoping Patrick Houlihan kept away from whiskey. When he stopped in to see her on Christmas morning, I invited him to have dinner with us, but he said his Ma would have his head if he didn't sit down at her table. I rather liked him for that. He came back in the evening, however, and delighted Kitty and Megan with stories about the horses he drove for Rupert's Brewery, while they, in turn, extolled the virtues of the pony up in Tarrytown.

It was later than usual when I finally had them tucked in, and when I went to bed myself shortly afterward, I felt as if I'd somehow been left out of things. . . .

Kitty woke up the next morning complaining that her throat hurt and burst into tears when she had difficulty swallowing bites of the pancakes Kathleen had made for breakfast. When I telephoned Dr. Sullivan, his nurse said he was away for the week but that his associate would see Kitty if I brought her to the office.

I asked Kathleen to let Mr. Heimlich know I'd be in later in the morning and bundled Kitty up in her warmest clothes. It was a cold, gray day, but fortunately the office was only two blocks away in a brownstone house on Thirtieth Street near Fourth Avenue. Kitty was still whimpering about not being able to eat anything as we trudged through patches of snow on the sidewalks, but once in the waiting room she sat quietly, leaning against me and eyeing the other patients.

At last the nurse showed us into the office, and when I saw the tall man standing behind a large mahogany desk, my heart skipped a beat. I must have been staring because he frowned and looked puzzled for a moment before his face broke into a delighted grin.

"Maud?" he asked. "It is Maud, isn't it? Maud grown up?"

"Dr. Tom!" I cried, disengaging myself from Kitty's grasp and going over to shake the warm, strong hand that had held mine in the hospital almost six years earlier. He came from behind the desk, and taking my hand in his, put his other arm around me and hugged me while an astonished Kitty stood looking at us.

"It's Kitty, Dr. Tom—" I began.

"Your daughter, Maud? Surely—"

"No, no. I'm not married. Kitty is my younger sister, and her throat—"

"I couldn't swallow my pancakes," Kitty interrupted.

"You couldn't, eh?" he said with a smile. "Well, we'll have to do something about that."

He won her over completely, talking quietly in the gentle voice I remembered so well while he examined her. When he finished, he took a package of lozenges from a small drawer and handed it to her.

"Suck on one of these, honey," he said. "It will make your

throat feel better. Now go outside with Miss Tierney while I talk to your sister."

He watched her go, then turned to me. "She has a bad throat, all right, and a few degrees of fever. Put her to bed, give her plenty of liquids, and I'll order some medication. I hope she's not coming down with measles, but there's a lot of it going around. If the rash appears, give me a call, and I'll come. Let me have the address—I knew it once. . . ."

He wrote it down on a prescription pad, then stood looking at me for a moment before opening the door to the waiting room.

"You've really grown up, Maud, and nicely, too," he said with a smile.

I felt myself blushing, but I would have been far more pleased with the compliment if I hadn't noticed the wedding band on the fourth finger of his left hand.

By the following morning it was apparent that Kitty did have the measles, and the next day Megan began to show symptoms. We had a bad two weeks. They both ran high fevers, making it necessary for Kathleen and me to be in constant attendance. There was no question of my going to the bookstore. Dr. Tom came every day, twice on the day Kitty's temperature rose to a hundred and five. I don't know what we would have done without him. We'd have managed, I suppose, but it would have been difficult without the confidence he inspired.

It was over at last, and the afternoon Dr. Tom pronounced the girls out of danger he sat down and had a cup of tea with me instead of rushing off to his next patient.

"You've had a hell of a time these past two weeks, Maud," he said, leaning forward to study my face. "You could do with a rest. Take a few days off—did you say you worked in a bookstore? I'm surprised you haven't found a handsome young husband to support you."

"No, I told you I wasn't married," I said slowly, "but I see that you are." I nodded toward his ring.

"I was," he said in a low voice, "but my wife died in childbirth. The baby didn't live either."

"Oh, I'm sorry."

"That's all right. It happened four years ago."

He went on to tell me that he'd left the hospital on North Brother Island shortly after I was discharged and moved to Boston. He'd worked in Massachusetts General Hospital until the past September when he decided to go into private practice.

"Dr. Sullivan is getting ready to retire. Did you know that? No? Well, he is, and I'll take over his practice, probably by the beginning of the summer. I didn't want to stay in Boston any longer—I'm a New Yorker—so here I am."

"I'm glad, Dr. Tom. You've been wonderful with Kitty and Megan."

"Maud, for God's sake, will you please drop the 'doctor'? You make me feel a hundred years old."

I laughed and said I'd try but that it would be hard to break a habit formed so long ago.

"I must be on my way," he said as he finished his tea. "I have a patient at Bellevue I ought to see. But look here—I've done all the talking, and I want to know more about you. What about dinner tomorrow night? You can safely leave the young ones now."

I don't think I stopped smiling for the rest of the day.

"I haven't tasted this since Mama died," I said, taking a sip of the dry sherry Tom ordered as soon as we were seated in the restaurant the next evening. "Papa used to pour a thimbleful for Angie and me on special occasions."

"I've often wondered," he said slowly, putting his glass down carefully, "whether I did the right thing in not telling you about your mother and brothers while you were in the hospital. When I talked to your sister on the phone, she thought it might be better to wait until you were home, but she left it up to me. . . ."

"It would have been the same shock either way," I said. "And what made it worse was Papa—his drinking and all."

"Tell me what went on," he said. "And don't try to spare me the details."

I told him everything I could remember about those awful days, and after I had described the dreadful scene in the parlor that resulted in Papa's death, I paused.

"Angie is responsible for his death, Tom, even if she didn't mean to kill him, and I perjured myself to protect her. No one else knows what happened. Kitty and Megan were too little to understand."

"Angie didn't murder him, Maud," he said, placing his hand over mine. "An accident like that could never be construed as murder. He was probably killing himself with alcohol anyway. And you didn't commit perjury. You weren't under oath, were you? No? Well then, put that out of your mind."

By the time the meal was over I had brought him up to date, and when I finished, he sat musing for a moment or two. When he did speak, it was to ask about Derek.

"Mr. Blauvelt certainly isn't the man you thought he was at first, is he, Maud?" he asked as we lingered over our coffee.

"No, not at all," I replied. "I misjudged him completely. In the beginning I thought he was a cold, austere person, someone who gave orders and expected them to be obeyed immediately and without question. And he may be like that in his business affairs, but I've come to realize that he's really a kind, considerate man and a very lonely one right now. Unfortunately I was influenced by what Angie said about him. You see, Tom, I saw very little of him until she disappeared. When he came looking for her that night, he was almost beside himself with worry; he seemed to be in a terrible rage, and I was afraid he'd become violent. After a while, though, when he'd calmed down and apologized, I realized that he was simply frantic because she'd left him, and ready to do anything to get her back.

"Poor Derek! He knows that she didn't love him. She married him for his money and then found that she couldn't stand living with him, so the picture she painted to me of him was distorted. One proof of that is that she quoted him as saying that if she left him, he would stop supporting Kitty and Megan and me. But he hasn't stopped."

"Of course, Maud, he could have threatened——"

"Perhaps, but I'm inclined to think she made that up."

"And you haven't heard from her in over a year?"

"A year and a half now—not since we left Tarrytown at the end of that first summer. But I'm not at all sure she wasn't in our house the following summer when we were away."

"Well, Angie doesn't need you to worry about her, honey. Women like her have a way of landing on their feet. Now, tell me about your job. How did you happen to find work in a bookstore?"

It had begun to snow while we were in the restaurant, and Tom wanted to send for a cab, but I said I'd been indoors so much that I'd rather walk, if he didn't mind.

"Will that muff keep your hands warm enough?" he asked as we set out.

"Oh, yes. It's sable. Derek gave it to me for Christmas."

"Oh, I see," he said, rather dryly I thought.

We were home in a matter of minutes. When I asked him if he'd like to come in, he said he'd better not, that he had an early appointment the next day. Then, after I'd thanked him for the dinner and said good night, he surprised me by asking rather diffidently if I was in love with Derek. He smiled when I said of course not, that Derek was a married man, and besides, he was old enough to be my father. Tom left then, and I went inside, wondering if I dared to hope that it wasn't just curiosity that prompted his question.

Long after Kitty and Megan had fully recovered, Tom continued to drop in several evenings a week "to check up on the young ones" and when he could spare the time, spend a half hour or so with me over a cup of cocoa. He liked to hear about my day at the bookstore, about Mr. Heimlich and Danny, and the habits of some of our eccentric customers. I remember how he laughed at the story of the richly dressed dowager who came in at least once a week for a French novel "for my sister, who is ill," she'd say in an apologetic way. Her sister had been ill for years, Mr. Heimlich said, and had very poor taste.

We were still chuckling over the dowager's transparent deception when Megan and Kitty came down in their nightgowns and begged Tom to come for dinner the next night. They were going to help Kathleen frost a great big cake for dessert, and they were sure he'd like it. When he accepted without hesitating a minute, I don't know who was happier, the children or I.

Shortly after I returned from work, he arrived with a bottle of sherry for me and a jar of hard candies for the girls.

"A glass of this will improve your appetite, Maud," he said as he opened the bottle. "You're still such a slip of a girl. You could use a few more pounds."

Perhaps the sherry did give me an appetite. Everything tasted particularly good that night, and Tom pronounced the cake frosting the best he had ever had. Afterward the four of us played Parcheesi until it was time for the girls to go up to bed, and since Tom left a few minutes later, I did not have much time alone with him. I was slightly consoled, however, by the thought that the hug he gave me when he was leaving was more than just a friendly one.

XVI

Derek returned from Europe in the middle of March, but we didn't see him for several weeks. He phoned to say he was back but that he'd picked up a nasty bronchial infection in London's damp, foggy weather and would stay away from us until he was sure he was cured.

"I'm sorry Uncle Derek is sick," Kitty said at breakfast after I'd told them about the phone call the night before. "I really am sorry, but I think Dr. Tom is more fun than Uncle Derek."

"He doesn't have a pony, though," Megan said thoughtfully.

"Mmmm, that's right," Kitty agreed. "Can I have another muffin, please?"

I was about to ask how many she'd already had when the phone rang. It was Tom calling to say he had two tickets for the Saturday matinee of *Sherlock Holmes* and would I like to see it?

"A grateful patient gave them to me, Maud. He has something to do with the production. I think you might like it.

William Gillette's a great actor—I've seen him before. And we could go someplace for dinner afterward."

I said I'd love it and immediately began to consider what to wear. I needn't have bothered, though; we never got there. I came close to never going anyplace again.

On Friday evening when I arrived home from the bookstore, Kathleen handed me a folded piece of paper that looked as if it had been torn from a child's copybook. My name and address were written in pencil on the outside, smudged but still legible.

"A little boy brought it, Miss Maud, as dirty a little rascal as I ever did see. He said a lady told him that if he delivered it, you'd pay him, so I gave him a quarter."

The message, written in what I recognized immediately as Angie's careless scrawl, was ominous:

Dear Maudie, I need help. Come to 591 Greenwich Street
as soon as you get this. Angie.

"What time did this come?" I asked Kathleen.

"About two o'clock this afternoon, Miss Maud. Should I have brought it over to the bookstore? He didn't say there was any hurry."

"No, no, it's all right, Kathleen, but I'll have to go out. Give Kitty and Megan their dinner, and save mine. I'll be back later."

I had no idea how to find the address Angie had given me, so I hurried over to the corner of Lexington Avenue and hailed a cab. Greenwich Street, I learned, runs north and south, west of lower Broadway, and 591 turned out to be in the middle of a block of run-down tenements northwest of Trinity Church. I heard later that the Corporation of Trinity Church was one of the largest landowners in the city and that it was subjected to severe criticism for the dreadful conditions that prevailed in its holdings. I still shudder when I think of what I saw that day.

I didn't think to have the cabdriver wait for me, but paid him off and hurried up the three sagging wooden steps to knock on the flimsy door. As I waited for someone to come, I noticed that a halfhearted attempt had been made to board up the broken window on my right and that on my left a dark alley led to the rear of the building. No one answered my knock, but when I pushed the rickety door open, I heard a querulous voice from somewhere in the depths of the house ask what I wanted.

"I'm looking for Angela Evans," I called out. "Which rooms are hers?"

The owner of the unpleasant voice appeared suddenly at the end of a dark, dirty hall holding the stub of a candle in one hand and using the other to support herself against the wall.

"Yer the second one today! Can't ye let a body have a drink in peace?"

All I could see by the dim light of the candle was the upper part of a thin, ill-clad female body and an emaciated toothless face half concealed by straggly wisps of gray hair, which she brushed away from her eyes before quickly reaching for the support of the wall.

"Angela Evans," I repeated. "Where are her rooms?"

"Don't know no Angela," she replied, "but if yer the one Billy took the letter to, it's right there."

She pointed to a door halfway down the hall, and muttering something that sounded like "Good riddance," retreated to her own quarters, slamming the door behind her with more force than I would have thought possible for such a skeleton. I wondered if Billy's quarter had been spent on gin.

My eyes were becoming accustomed to the darkness, but still I had to feel my way to the second door on the right, which swung open of its own accord when I touched it. I groped frantically for a handkerchief to hold to my nose against the horrible stench that greeted me as I entered a squalid chamber and peered around at the wretched furnishings. There was no window, and the only light came from a single gas jet on the far wall. In the center of the room a small table held a few pieces of crockery, a couple of spoons, and a carving knife, or maybe it was a bread knife—I didn't look closely. A broken wooden chair had been knocked over. An old stove stood in one corner, but I could see no sink, no door that might lead to a bathroom—and at first, no occupant.

When I turned, however, to examine the darkest part of the room, farthest from the gas jet, I saw a bed of sorts and what looked like the outline of a sleeping figure. I called Angie's name softly, so as not to startle her, and moved toward the makeshift bed. It wasn't she. It was a young bearded man, who lay on his back in a tangle of bloodstained bedclothes. I was staring down into a pair of wide-open lifeless eyes when I heard a voice behind me. I whipped around and immediately tried to back away from the burly-looking fellow who stood there smiling at me.

"She sent me to fetch you before your husband comes, miss," he said slowly. "She phoned him to tell him to get you, but I guess she changed her mind—or maybe he couldn't come—"

"What—who are you?" I gasped. "What are you talking about?"

" 'Don't come back without her,' she said. 'Use force if'—"

I tried to run to the open door, but he grabbed me, and a moment later a sack or something like it enveloped my head and shoulders. Strong arms picked me up, and I could feel myself being carried outside and put into a vehicle of some sort. My muffled screams attracted no attention, but when I kept struggling, my captor pressed something against my face, and I lost consciousness.

Some time later—I had no idea how long I'd been unconscious—I awoke in a bed in a strange room to see Mrs. Williams sitting in a nearby chair. She was talking to a man who stood close to the door, and I quickly shut my eyes again so she wouldn't know I was awake.

"You're a bigger fool than I thought possible, Robert," she was saying. "How could you make such a mistake? Couldn't you see that she isn't Angélique? This one is her scrawny little sister. Why—"

"How was I to tell one from the other, Cora?" he asked petulantly. "Dark in there, it was. And you said to bring her back no matter what. Why did you want her here when you'd phoned her husband to go for her?"

"Because I changed my mind!" she snapped. "Because I can get more out of him if I hold her here. And he'd pay. He'd pay anything to get her back."

They were quiet for a moment or two before Mrs. Williams spoke again.

"Well, Robert, we can't use this one. How do you propose to get rid of her?"

The man's reply made my blood run cold. He spoke in a low tone, and I didn't catch the first part of what he said, but I distinctly heard "there's always the river." He laughed then, a short barking laugh. "Or put her back where I found her with the dead guy—"

"What! Did you kill—come with me, Robert! At once!"

At that point I heard the door open and close and the sound of a key being turned in the lock. I waited a minute or two before opening my eyes again. When I was sure the room was empty, I sat up and tried to take stock of the situation. My head ached slightly, and my heart was pounding, but I seemed to be unharmed. I was fully dressed except for my shoes, which I found next to the bed when I threw off the comforter that covered me and stood up.

The room was elaborately furnished, with tasseled valences surmounting the deep-red velvet drapes on the two windows, a red-and-gold figured carpet, and heavy silk bed hangings. The chair Mrs. Williams had been sitting in was upholstered in gold velvet, and long gold fringe hung from the shades of the lamps on the dresser. I was about to open the drapes—I had a wild idea of escaping through a window—when I heard the key in the lock again.

A young girl in a maid's uniform came in, looked at me, smiled, and without a word went out again, locking the door behind her. She's gone to tell Mrs. Williams I'm awake, I thought with a shiver, wondering what was coming next.

Apparently Angie had been in this place, whatever it was, and had left. That she was wanted back was evident from what Mrs. Williams had said to the man Robert. I couldn't imagine what my sister was doing there or why she had left such luxurious quarters for the filthy hovel on Greenwich Street. Then, with a start, I remembered the dead man and sat stone still, thoroughly bewildered and even more thoroughly frightened.

When the maid returned with a tray of food, I asked her to please leave the door open so that I could leave. She smiled and nodded but did not reply. She simply put the tray down and turned to leave the room as Mrs. Williams appeared in the doorway.

XVII

When the tall woman entered the room, I backed away until I was up against the footboard of the bed. She was still wearing her customary black, but instead of the severe, unadorned cotton dress of the housekeeper, her gown that night was one of heavy silk taffeta that swished when she walked. The gems at her throat and in her ears sparkled, but they emphasized rather than softened the hard lines of her face, and the delicate diamond (or rhinestone?) bracelets on her strong wrists looked out of place.

"Sit down," she commanded, "and listen to me. No harm will come to you if you do as I say. Otherwise . . ."

I perched rather than sat on the edge of the bed, feeling like a trapped animal while I waited for her to continue. She was silent for a good sixty seconds, maybe longer, leaving me to imagine what the "otherwise" meant—the river? Was the East River to claim me, after all?

"As I told you once before," she said finally, "your sister is indebted to me, and I *will* be repaid. It has taken me over a year to track her down, and now she has eluded me. I know that she *was* at five ninety-one Greenwich Street, and I also know that you went to see her—''

''I didn't see her,'' I said quietly. ''She wasn't there.''

''But you had reason to believe you'd find her there, didn't you. Or you wouldn't have been there yourself.''

''She wrote me a note.''

''Where is it?'' she asked sharply.

''In my coat pocket. Where is my coat? And my purse? And why—''

''I will ask the questions,'' she snapped, ''and you will answer them. Do you know where she is?''

''No.''

''Why did she send for you?''

''She said she needed help.''

''And you gave her money, a large sum, and she took off—''

''No, no! I told you I didn't see her. Oh! You're hurting me! Let go of my wrist!''

She released her hold and turned away for a moment. When she looked at me again, I felt as if those fierce dark eyes of hers were boring into my skull, but I stared back, trying not to quiver.

''Very well,'' she said, still not taking her eyes off me. ''I will give you twelve hours to make up your mind to tell me where she is.''

''Even if I knew where she was, and told you, I'm sure Angie has no money to pay you, but I could give you—''

''How much?''

''A thousand dollars,'' I said carefully, remembering Derek's stricture.

''Not enough. Not nearly enough, and if your sister has no funds, she will have to work off her debt. That is all there is to it. Now, as I said before, you have twelve hours in which to decide to cooperate with me. I have had food brought to

117

you, and there are nightclothes in the closet. Eat, then go to bed. Let's hope you'll be more reasonable after a night's sleep."

With that she left, and once more I was locked in. Sleep, of course, was out of the question, and after washing my hands and face in the small bathroom that adjoined the room, I wrapped myself in the comforter and sat in the gold chair, wondering what Mrs. Williams meant by "reasonable." Should I make up something about Angie's whereabouts and send my captors off on a wild-goose chase? I thought I might be able to gain some time by such a ruse, but what would happen afterward? What would she do, or have Robert do, to me? I don't know when I'd felt so terror-stricken, so incapable of logical thought, and after a while I simply sat still, staring at the locked door.

There was no clock in the room, so I had no idea of the time, and I don't know how long I had been sitting huddled under the comforter when I heard the sound of the key being turned slowly in the lock. I sprang up, not knowing what to expect, too frightened to scream or call out. I relaxed somewhat when I saw the same maid who had come earlier standing quite still in the doorway, with her finger to her lips. She smiled, and taking one of my hands in hers, indicated that I should go with her. For some reason I trusted her and putting my shoes on, nodded that I would follow her. At that point almost anything seemed better than remaining locked up in that strange room.

We went swiftly along a thickly carpeted hall to a rear staircase, one used by the servants, I guessed, at which point she took off her shoes and motioned to me to do the same. I saw why in a moment. The steps there were of bare wood and would have been noisy. Since they were unlighted she held my hand again and guided me down two flights. She paused at the bottom in what looked like a small entryway and listened.

There was no sound, and after we put our shoes on, she eased a heavy door open, and we stepped out into the cold, windy night.

I had no idea which direction we were going in or where we were headed as my companion led the way through a series of alleys and open spaces, but she seemed to know what she was doing, and I followed her willingly. When we emerged on a city sidewalk—it turned out to be Twenty-second Street— she paused and put her arm around my shoulders.

"I had no chance to get your coat, miss, nor my own for that matter, but we're safely out of there now. Tell me, where do you live? I hope to God it's not far off."

I told her, and as we hurried through the dark streets past the beggars sleeping in the doorways of unlighted houses, I asked her who she was and why she had rescued me.

"I'm Ellen Grady, miss, and as glad to get out of there as you are. Sure and I'll explain later. Right now, it's gettin' you home before you catch your death of cold I'm thinkin' about."

The first faint light of morning was just visible when I rang the bell at Thirty-second Street, hoping Kathleen would hear it. The door was flung open almost at once, and I stumbled into Tom's outstretched arms.

"Bring Ellen in," I murmured as he carried me into the parlor and put me down gently on the sofa. "Without her, I wouldn't be here."

Tom nodded and told me to lie quietly until I felt rested. I remember that he made me drink something and let me hold his hand until I fell asleep. When I opened my eyes again, the sun was streaming in the parlor windows, and he was sitting in Papa's old easy chair watching me.

"This reminds me of the time I woke up in the hospital and saw you smiling at me, Tom," I said. "Do you remember that?"

"Indeed I do, honey. How do you feel?"

"As if I need a bath and a change of clothes," I said. "But, Tom, I have to tell you—oh, where's Ellen? And I'll have to tell Derek—"

"Not now, honey. First breakfast, then a bath. I have a few calls to make, but I'll be back, and then we'll talk. Ellen's in the kitchen with Kathleen, by the way. They seem to have hit it off."

"How did you happen to be here, Tom?"

"Kathleen was worried when you weren't home by midnight and called me. I came over, but decided to wait until morning before notifying the police—oh, Maud, darling—"

He leaned over, and my arms went around his neck as he kissed me gently on the lips.

Kitty and Megan, not surprisingly, were satisfied when I told them I'd been out to dinner with a friend and was late coming in. They were more interested in the ferryboat ride Kathleen had promised to take them on that afternoon than in my affairs. I wasn't too happy about letting them make the trip across the harbor to Staten Island, but my common sense told me that it would be unfair to forbid it because of my own frightening experience. I know it's foolish of me, but to this day I am fearful of traveling on the water and avoid it whenever possible.

"Begin at the beginning, honey," Tom said as soon as they left and we were sitting in the parlor with Ellen. "You came home from the bookstore a little after five and found the note from Angie. . . ."

He listened without interrupting, nodding his head from time to time.

"It sounds to me as if you spent the night—or part of it—in a high-class brothel, honey," he said when I finished speaking.

"A what?" I was aghast.

"Yes, miss," Ellen said. "That's what it is, and I was as

dumbfounded as yourself when I found out. I'd just come from Ireland, you see. I wasn't off the boat ten minutes when she hired me. Said it was a place for a maid in a private residence.''

"How long were you there, Ellen?'' Tom asked.

"Too long, sir. Three months, thereabouts. Oh, I tried any number of times to leave, but she caught me, or Robert did, and the things they threatened me with—I was that scared, being in a strange country and all. Then they brought you in, miss, and I heard them say you were Miss Angélique's sister—that's when I made up my mind.

"You see, miss, before you came, I'd been figuring and planning what to do. I watched where Robert put the keys. He has a closet near the pantry. When he was up there in the room with you and her, I unlocked the back door we came out of, praying to God that he wouldn't check it later. He got drunk, though, after the madame gave him a piece of her mind for bringing you instead of Miss Angélique. So when I was sure he was dead to the world, I went up to get you—''

"You knew Angie, then? How long was she there, Ellen?'' I asked.

"I don't rightly know, miss. Only a few days, I think. She was that beautiful, and so sweet. But she went away, slipped past Robert, I heard. And what a ruckus that caused! The madame was in a terrible state, that she was. Said she'd find her if she had to turn the city inside out.''

"Tom, you remember that I told you Mrs. Williams said Angie was indebted to her when she came here looking for her? She said it again last night. Derek thinks Angie borrowed money from her—''

"It's obvious,'' he said slowly, "that the woman has some hold over Angie. Did she keep her locked up, Ellen?''

"I couldn't say for sure, sir. I don't think so, though, because once or twice I saw her in the hall, and when she sent for me to help her hook up a dress, the door was open.''

"Do you know how long Mrs. Williams had been there when she hired you, Ellen?" I asked.

"Not really, miss, but I don't think it was very long from what I heard from Cook and the other maids. Seems she came to take care of her sister, Madame Pauline, who owned the place. Very sick Madame Pauline was, and when she died, Mrs. Williams was the boss. And quite different she was, too, the girls said. Madame Pauline was one for fun and laughs, always singin' and all, and everyone liked her. But Mrs. Williams was another story, sour as a lemon, never a smile on her. They were all afraid of her, even Robert in spite of his bein' her brother. And you know what a big man he is."

"I had only a glimpse of him, Ellen," I said, "but I didn't like what I saw. What were his duties?"

"Oh, he was a kind of guard, watchin' out that the wrong kind of gentlemen didn't come in. I saw him put one out once. And any repair work was his, like fixin' a broken pipe or that. Always after him Mrs. Williams was, sendin' him on errands and scoldin' him when he got things wrong. He wasn't too bright Robert wasn't. Didn't have enough sense to get out.

"He'd get drunk, too, and then she'd threaten to send him away, but she never did. Afraid she'd not find anyone else to do her dirty work for her, most-like."

"Did you see him carry Miss Maud in, Ellen?" Tom asked.

"No, sir, that I didn't. It must have been our dinnertime when she came. The servants' dining room is in the back, next to the kitchen, but I know that Robert had to have his meal later that night. Then it was much later when he got drunk. Mrs. Williams will hand him his head this time, for sure!"

"How many women were there, Ellen?" I asked.

"There were nine, miss, not counting Miss Angélique— none as beautiful as she was, but each one with her regulars—I mean, the same men coming to see them. Once in a while a stranger came, someone from out of town, but he had to be recommended, I heard."

"Did Angie—I mean, Miss Angélique—have her regulars?"

"Oh no, miss. She wasn't there long enough."

"Was that her room I was in, Ellen?"

"Oh, no. She had the best room in the place, all white and gold. You were in a room that was sort of extra, a spare room, like."

Tom must have noticed that I was close to tears at that point because he leaned over and took my hand in his as he turned to Ellen.

"How did you know so much about the alleys you took Miss Maud through, Ellen, if you hadn't been able to get out?"

"From the winders, sir. I'd pretend to be polishin' the glass, and all the while I was studying how to get away. Mighty clean, those back winders were," she said with a slight smile.

Her story had the ring of truth to it, and Tom, evidently satisfied that she was honorable, asked me if she could stay with us while he looked around for a job for her.

"Oh, would you be so kind, sir? I'm needin' work, I am. I've a bit saved up," she said, patting the pocket of her skirt, "but t'won't last long. Stingy with her wages she was."

We were quiet for a few moments, and then Ellen, sensing that I wanted to talk to Tom privately, said she'd promised Kathleen to clean the vegetables for dinner and excused herself.

"What should I do now, Tom?" I asked when we were alone. "Angie's in trouble and needs—"

"Tell me again about the room on Greenwich Street, honey. Number five-nine-one, you said?"

"Yes, but Tom, don't go there! Angie's not there, and a dead man—"

"Yes, I know. But are you sure he was dead?"

"Quite sure. He was all bloody, and I'm afraid Angie might have—oh, I don't know—the woman who pointed out her room to me said I was the second person to ask for her, so maybe—"

"No maybe about it. Someone was there before you. From your description, the dead man had probably been in a fight and was dumped there. We may never know, but I think you'll hear from Angie again, Maud, and if you do and she asks you to meet her, don't go alone. Call me any time of the day or night, and I'll go with you. Promise?"

He also made me promise to see that the house was properly locked up, and that the chains were on before I went upstairs. "And get to bed early tonight, honey," he said, standing up and pulling me to my feet. He held me at arm's length for a moment, then gave me a quick kiss just as the front door burst open and the excited chatter of the returning ferryboat riders could be heard in the hall.

Early on Sunday morning Tom phoned to see how I was and to say that in spite of my plea to stay away from Greenwich Street, he had gone there after leaving me the day before.

"I thought there was a chance that the man you saw might be unconscious, Maud, in which case I'd get him to the hospital in the hope that if he recovered, we might be able to learn something about Angie."

"Was he alive?"

"No. By the time I arrived, the room was empty, and the boy who was hanging around the front of the house, probably the same one who delivered the note to you, told me a dead man had been taken off to the morgue that morning in a police wagon."

"Did he know who the man was?"

"Just that his name was Greg, nothing more. And he ran off before I could ask more questions. Then I decided to check the city morgue. I know John Herkimer, one of the pathologists there, and he arranged for me to see the corpse. I'd say he was between twenty-five and thirty, dark-haired, dark-eyed, not bad-looking. He'd been stabbed in the jugular, and he had no identification whatsoever. No one's come forward to claim the body, either. Herkimer says they get a couple of corpses a week from that neighborhood, sometimes people who've starved or frozen to death, and sometimes ones who've been killed in a fight.

"So I'm afraid we don't have much to go on, honey, but I'll see what I can find out about the brothel. Ellen gave me the address. Don't get your hopes up, Maud. Those places pay heavily for protection. The cops on the beat get their share, and so do some of the higher-ups, and they're not apt to jeopardize the additional income. But there's no harm in trying. One more thing about the room on Greenwich Street—did you see any sign of clothing or possessions? A suitcase? Anything?"

"No, nothing."

"Perhaps Angie had gone to pick up their things just after she wrote the note and expected to be back by the time you arrived. Well, anyway—I'll see what I can find out at the brothel. Give it a try at least."

He did try, but nothing came of it. The investigator he hired reported that both Mrs. Williams and Robert adamantly denied having heard of an Angela or an Angélique and threatened to call the police if he didn't leave at once.

That was Monday. On Wednesday I suggested that Tom and I both confront Mrs. Williams, although everything pointed to the fact that she knew no more than I about Angie's whereabouts. Tom agreed to accompany me, and by eight o'clock that evening we were ringing the bell of the house on Twenty-first Street. When Robert opened the door I was afraid he'd recognize me, but either he hadn't been very observant or he'd been drinking because he gave no sign of having seen me before.

We were still standing in the vestibule when a cheerful voice called out from one of the rooms: "Who is it, *mon brave?* A gentleman to see someone in particular?"

A moment later, a plump, smiling woman with a mass of bright-gold hair piled high above a heavily made-up face appeared at Robert's side. She was dressed for the evening in a low-cut gown of red silk trimmed with gold lace and with diamond sunbursts on each shoulder.

"What are you doing here, *ma petite?*" she asked, looking at me. "The gentleman I can take care of, but—"

"We'd like to have a few words with Mrs. Williams," Tom interrupted. "May we come in?"

"Ah, Mrs. Williams!" she exclaimed. "Yes, of course, do come in. Here in the parlor." She led us into a small but expensively furnished room to the right of the hall.

"I am sure I can do for you whatever Mrs. Williams could have done," she said.

We remained standing, looking at her, and I noticed that she was casting appraising glances at Tom, ignoring me completely.

" 'Could have done'?" I asked. "Where is Mrs. Williams?"

"Alas, *ma petite,* she was a friend of yours, no? Where she is I do not know. She has sold out to me, just yesterday, and she is gone. And she did not say where she was going. I did not think it wise to ask, either, from her manner, you know. In my business one must know how to read the signals."

"You mean she suddenly decided to sell the place yesterday?" Tom asked.

"It was not so sudden, my friend. For months now, ever since Madame Pauline died, I have been trying to buy this house, and only on Monday did she agree to sell to me. Then yesterday I paid her—I had the money at hand—and she gave me a receipt and the deed and took herself away. I have not yet had time to make any changes, but there will be some.'' She lowered her voice. ''That Robert, for one, will have to go. *Très stupide!* He strikes the wrong note for a high-class establishment. In the meantime we are open for business as usual.'' She smiled and looked at Tom expectantly.

''I'm afraid we've taken enough of your time,'' he said, taking my arm and turning toward the door.

''Not at all, not at all,'' she said jovially. ''Come any time, sir, but perhaps it would be wise to leave your friend at home the next time.''

We lost no time in leaving, and once outside, I asked him what he thought Mrs. Williams was up to now.

''I think she smelled trouble, Maud, and panicked. Maybe the investigator scared her. She and her henchman may have had something to do with the murder on Greenwich Street—and of course she could be charged with kidnapping in your case. She's probably gone out of town, or into hiding. There's one good thing, though: she won't be after Angie anymore, now that she's sold the business.''

''I'm not so sure,'' I said. ''She wants the money she lent to Angie, and I don't think she'll give up easily. I'm afraid she might harm Angie.''

''Look, honey, you *must* stop worrying. We've done everything we can think of. If Angie still needs help, she'll get in touch with you again, and then we'll decide what to do. And, as I said before, women like Angie are generally capable of taking care of themselves.''

Angie *was* resourceful, I knew that, but even so . . .

XVIII

I marveled that Mr. Heimlich kept me on when I'd been absent from the bookstore so much. He could easily have found someone else. My story about being kidnapped (an abridged version) might have sounded like an outrageous fabrication to another man, but it horrified him and led to much headshaking and mutterings about what the world was coming to. Danny was equally shocked and insisted on seeing me safely home each evening for several weeks after the incident.

They were happy weeks for me in spite of my concern for Angie. I heard from Tom daily. On the nights he was out on a call or at the hospital and couldn't stop by, he'd phone to make sure I was all right, and three or four times during those weeks we had quiet dinners by ourselves at one of his favorite restaurants.

When I asked him how he happened to be familiar with so many eating places, he laughed and said he preferred them to the food Dr. Sullivan's cook prepared.

"As you know," he went on, "my flat is in the house next door to the office, and I have a standing invitation to join the

Sullivans for dinner whenever I choose. I do dine with them on occasion—they're such a warmhearted family—but I can stand just so much boiled beef and vegetables, a favorite of theirs. I much prefer this.'' He nodded at the poached salmon the waiter had put in front of us.

"I've been here before," I said, looking around at the plain tablecloths and the candles in pewter holders. "Derek brought me.''

"Derek? When?"

"Last November, just before he sailed.''

"Did he bring you here often?" he asked casually, applying himself to his salmon.

"Oh, no. Just that once. Why, Tom?''

"Just wondering. Would you care for some more of this sauce?''

He was unusually quiet as we walked home after the meal and then surprised me by asking if he could come in for a few minutes. I wondered what was on his mind because he usually just saw me inside and went on his way after a quick good-night kiss.

The children were already in bed, and Kathleen, who had waited up for me, said she'd go on up if we didn't need her.

"How is Ellen doing, Kathleen?" Tom asked. He'd found a position for her in the household of one of his medical friends. "Do you ever see her?''

"Oh yes, sir. She's fine she is. She comes over on her day off. I think she likes it here, Miss Maud. I was thinkin', too, maybe after Pat and I are married, you might see your way clear to havin' her. She thinks the world of you, Ellen does.''

"We'll see about it, Kathleen," I said. "But don't say anything about it to her yet.''

"Not a word, miss," she said with a happy smile, and left the parlor.

Tom was standing in front of the dying coal fire looking at

me, and when he heard a door close upstairs, he came across the room and took me in his arms.

"Ellen's not the only one to think the world of you, Miss Maud," he said huskily. "I know I'm not old enough to be your father, but I *am* ten years older than you—does that matter? I love you. I love you—I want to marry you."

When I told him I'd been in love with him since the day he first held my hand in the hospital, his eyes lighted up, and a moment later he carried me over to the sofa where he held me close to him as he rained kisses on my face and neck.

XIX

I waited until Derek said he was feeling fit again before telling him about the brothel, Greenwich Street, and Mrs. Williams. He came on a rainy Sunday evening early in April when Tom was with me, bringing little French dolls for Kitty and Megan and a vial of perfume for me. He was surprised when I told him Tom and I were to be married in May but congratulated Tom heartily, wished me happiness, and asked what our plans were. At that point we hadn't made many definite ones, but we talked about possible ones, with suggestions from the girls until their bedtime.

After they went reluctantly upstairs, I glanced at Tom and, seeing him nod, I said rather hesitantly that we had news of a sort about Angie.

"Yes? What news?" Derek sat bolt upright and fastened his eyes on me.

Between us, Tom and I left nothing out, beginning with the delivery of Angie's note and ending with my rescue by Ellen Grady. When Derek heard that according to Ellen, Angie had been part of Mrs. Williams's establishment, the color drained from his face, and he gripped the arms of his chair so hard that his knuckles turned white. I thought he might be about to faint and ran to get him a glass of brandy, but when I offered it to him, he stared, unseeing, across the room.

"Give him time, Maud," Tom said softly. "The shock—"

"In the arms of other men!" Derek shouted. "Anything but that! I can stand anything but that! If I knew who they were, I'd—" He broke off, as if he suddenly realized he was not alone, and carefully picked up the brandy I had placed on the table next to him.

He drank it slowly, and then, resting his head on the back of the chair, closed his eyes. "Please accept my apologies," he said after a few minutes of complete silence. "My behavior—"

"Completely understandable, old man," Tom said. "No need for an apology."

Derek glanced at him gratefully, then turned to me. "You weren't hurt, were you, Maud?" he asked, his face full of concern.

"No," Tom answered for me. "She wasn't hurt, just half frightened to death."

"Oh, my God! Are you sure you're all right, Maud? I'm so sorry—I'm to blame for all this. I never should have married her. . . ." Once again he broke off and stared down at his hands, which he kept clasping and unclasping.

"You're not any more to blame than Angie is," Tom said calmly. "If she should return to you—"

"No," Derek said sharply, "that won't ever work. I've explained to Maud how I feel. I yearn for Angela in my heart, but my head tells me that I would never be able to live with her again. However, I will provide for her. I cannot let her live in poverty. Luxury meant so much to her. . . ."

He didn't stay long after that. He asked me to phone him if I heard from Angie again, and then he left, taking with him the unused checkbook he had given me before going to Europe.

"I can't tell you how sorry I am you've been involved in all this, Maud," he said as I saw him to the door. "If I could only get my hands on that Williams woman! But that's neither here nor there. Good night, my dear. I'm happy that your future is in such good hands."

When I returned to the parlor, Tom drew me down on the sofa beside him so that I could rest my head on his shoulder.

"You're right, honey," he said after a moment or two. "He's still in love with her. Poor guy—he's torn between loving her and hating her, and it's going to take time for him to get over her, if he ever does."

"Do you think it's likely that he will? He seemed so miserable."

"And unstable. His rage almost got the better of him when he thought of Angie in another man's arms. I was all set to put a hammerlock on him if it got out of control. The potential for violence is there, all right."

When he felt me shudder, he held me close to him, then closer. It was late when he left me.

The day I arrived at the bookstore wearing the ring Tom had given me the night before, Mr. Heimlich held his head in his hands and moaned that he'd known all along that it was too good to last. But, he said, despite my treachery, unfaithfulness, and ingratitude, he wished me happiness, and said he'd let me go without a fuss if I promised to drop in once in a while.

Danny said my "feller" must be all right since he'd had the imagination to give me an emerald instead of the customary diamond, but he wished I'd waited until he'd at least come to the climax of the opus.

"I'm only up to chapter ten, Maud, and still have a long way to go, probably ten more."

They were both astounded when I said I had not planned to leave, not for the present anyway.

"You're not leaving? What will your feller say to that?"

"He said he thought it was a good idea, that I'm not the type to sit home and sew a fine seam," I replied. "I'll need some time off in May, though, for the wedding, but since I won't be going to Tarrytown this summer, I'll be able to come here. That should help you get on with a chapter or two, Danny."

"Look at her, Mr. Heimlich," Danny exclaimed. "Look at her face! I've read about a person looking radiant but never did see one. Now I know how it looks. I think I'll put you in my book, Maud."

I hadn't known it showed, but I did know I'd never been as happy as I was that spring. Nothing was as important as the thought that Tom loved me—I felt like hugging myself every time I thought of him. I was even able to forget about Angie for days at a time while Tom and I made plans, changed them, and made new ones.

When I told him I had thought about letting Kitty, Megan, and Kathleen spend the summer at Blauvelt House again—I was sure Derek would want them—so that we could have the house to ourselves for a while, Tom shook his head.

"Derek's been good to you, Maud," he said when he saw how puzzled I looked. "He's been *very* good to you, but from now on, you're *my* family, to be supported by me. I don't have the Blauvelt wealth, but I have plenty, and I'd rather you didn't accept anything more from Derek. Besides, I'm not at all keen about leaving Kitty and Megan in his care just now. I'm not sure how good his control over his emotions is. But don't worry, honey. I'll have a talk with Derek. He'll understand."

I knew Tom was right, and I thought Derek would understand, but I couldn't help wondering if he wouldn't be disappointed when he learned that none of us would be with him in Tarrytown for the summer. Kitty and Megan were to go to a girls' camp in the mountains, one to which Tom's sister, Louise, had sent her daughters for several summers, and of course I would stay in the city with him.

On the other hand, it occurred to me that perhaps Derek, who still did not look too well, might be relieved that he was not to have two active little girls on his hands for the better part of three months, even if it did mean he'd have some lonely hours. At that point, though, there was much that I didn't know, never could have imagined. . . .

We were married quietly on the twenty-first of May, and after two weeks spent in a rambling old-fashioned inn on Cape Cod, we settled down to a prolonged honeymoon in the city. For once, the hot summer days slipped by almost too quickly. In earlier years I had looked forward eagerly to the end of summer, to the excitement of going back to school, to the crisp days of fall, to what I still think of as the beginning of the year, but in 1910 I experienced no such longing. Several of Tom's patients were away, so he wasn't overworked, and business at the bookstore was so slow that Mr. Heimlich told me to take Saturdays off. We gave Kathleen a vacation for the month of July, and when she returned at the beginning of August, she asked if she could just come in by the day until the children came home.

"My mum broke her leg, Miss Maud," she said, "and could use a little help right now. So if you could see your way to doin' without me evenings, I'll leave the dinner ready for you to serve, and then I'll be home in time to help Mum cook. And you can leave the dishes. I'll wash them up in the mornin'."

Once in a while Tom would be home ahead of me, waiting in the dim light of the parlor where the shades had been drawn against the sun until he heard my key in the door. But in general I was the first one to return from work. I have to smile to myself, even today, at the memory of one hot, humid afternoon in particular. I thought I had plenty of time to bathe and dress before Tom came in since he'd said that morning that he might be delayed at the hospital. I heard the front door open, though, while I was still dallying in a tub full of cool, refreshing water. I called out to him that I would be down in a few minutes, but a moment later he put his head around the partially open door, smiled, knelt down, and bathed me carefully, tenderly. We were extremely late having dinner that night.

"Would you mind moving to another house, honey?" Tom asked me at breakfast one Saturday morning. "One in which I could have my office?"

"Do you mean Dr. Sullivan's house?"

"No, no. It's not for sale, and we'd want more room. I was thinking of a double brownstone. That way, I wouldn't have to usurp the entire parlor floor for an office and a waiting room. What do you say?"

"I wouldn't mind moving at all," I answered, looking around the familiar dining room. "A new house would be exciting. I don't dislike this one, but for the past six years I haven't been particularly happy in it—until recently, that is."

"Right," he said, smiling as he rose from his chair and came around the table to kiss me. "I've a patient to see, but I'll be home in plenty of time to take you out to lunch, and then we can start looking around."

After that, we spent several Saturday and Sunday afternoons checking various neighborhoods, and it was on one of those occasions that I saw for the first time the fountain in Tompkins Square Park that had been erected a few years earlier and dedicated to the victims of the *General Slocum* disaster. We paused in front of it for a few minutes, and on our way home

Tom asked me how long it had taken me to get over the shock of my mother's and brothers' deaths.

"I don't know, exactly," I answered slowly. "Sometimes I think the conditions I found at home shocked me almost enough to drive the deaths out of my mind. Of course I missed Mama terribly and cried myself to sleep for weeks. I missed the boys too, especially Johnnie, but Angie and I were so busy, and so afraid of Papa—of what he might do—that there was little time to brood during the daytime. Perhaps it's a ridiculous thing to say, but I think that in a strange way the second shock helped me get over the first one."

"Not ridiculous at all, honey. Sometimes when a patient is sick with something we can't pinpoint and then comes down with something we know we can cure, the treatment of the second illness cures the first one. In your case, dealing with the situation at home kept your mind off the deaths until enough time went by so that they receded into the past. And I think once I get you into a different house—oh, here we are."

He stooped to pick up the evening paper the newsboy had tossed onto the top step and then unlocked the door. The telephone rang as soon as we were inside, and a moment later Tom was on his way to the hospital to see a patient who had suddenly taken a turn for the worse.

After he left, I set out the cold supper Kathleen had prepared for us and was about to go upstairs to change into a cooler dress when a headline in the newspaper caught my eye. I sat down slowly and read that Derek Andrus Blauvelt, prominent New York financier and well-known philanthropist, had been found dead at his estate in Tarrytown. An investigation was in progress, but no details were available at the present time.

XX

Since Derek had not looked well the last time we saw him for dinner ("liverish," Tom said), we had no reason to attribute his death to other than natural causes until *The New York Times* arrived Sunday morning. A column on the front page informed us that he'd been stabbed in the throat on Friday afternoon as he lay resting on the leather couch in the study where he once spent so much time. The weapon, thought to be a dagger or an awl, had not been found, and the police had not determined the identity of the murderer.

The members of the staff—the housekeeper, cook, maids, chauffeur, and gardener—had no knowledge of any visitors on Friday, nor had they seen a stranger on the premises. As far as anyone knew, nothing was missing, which seemed to rule out robbery as a motive. Police were anxious to interview Mr. Blauvelt's wife, the former Angela Evans, who, the staff said, was traveling abroad.

The authorities were continuing their investigation.

Poor Derek, I thought after the first shock of the brutal murder had subsided a bit. He couldn't bring himself to admit publicly that Angie had left him and had given it out that she was on a pleasure trip to Europe. I hoped she *was* abroad, but when I remembered her note and that squalid room on Greenwich Street, I nearly cried out.

"It must be the same person," I said to Tom, "the one who killed the man in Greenwich Street—and oh, Tom! Angie was connected with both him and Derek! Who else—"

"It can't be Angie, honey," he said. "It takes strength to drive a knife into a man's throat, and from your description of Angie, slender and fragile-looking, I'm sure she wouldn't be physically capable—"

"Oh, I *know* Angie couldn't have done it—absolutely not—but Tom, think of this: She did kill my father, and even though it was accidental, she was responsible for his death. And her life since she left Derek has obviously been strange, and probably not easy. I've told you how much she loved luxury. She may have become desperate in her search for it, and since she'd killed once and gotten away with it, she may have thought she'd inherit Derek's wealth, and wouldn't care if she killed again. Also she was completely familiar with Blauvelt House and Derek's habits, and could have slipped in unobserved. And one more thing—she definitely was in the room on Greenwich Street. That's where she sent the note from. . . . I don't believe any of this for a minute, but can't you see what a strong case could be made against her if the police knew as much as we do?"

"Of course I can see it, honey, and when they get to us—oh yes, they will come here—all we have to do is answer their questions. We do not have to volunteer anything that might point to Angie. And remember this: The police do not know that Angie killed your father."

I was on edge all day, expecting the police to arrive at any moment, but it was not until the following evening, when fortunately Tom was at home, that a detective appeared at the door.

He introduced himself as Lieutenant Moran and said he wouldn't take up much of our time. He was a big man, heavy but not fat, neatly dressed in a dark suit and surprisingly soft-spoken. "I have just a few questions," he said, taking a notebook from his pocket and looking at me. "I understand, Mrs. Cavanaugh, that Angela Evans Blauvelt is your sister. Is that correct?"

When I nodded, he asked when I had last seen her.

"It was about this time two years ago, at the end of August," I answered, "when my younger sisters and I left Blauvelt House to return here. She was standing on the portico, waving good-bye to us."

"You haven't seen her for two years? Your sister?" he asked.

"No, but that's not as unusual as it sounds," I said, trying to choose my words carefully. "Once Angie married Derek, her life was completely different from mine. They moved in different circles entirely. I was up there that summer only because she hadn't been well and couldn't go out in society. Derek thought she was lonesome, and that my company would do her good."

"I see," he said, making a note in his book. "Did she and Mr. Blauvelt go abroad frequently?"

"Yes, they did. Derek had business in London and Paris, and she'd go with him."

"And your sister is in Europe now?"

"According to the newspapers, yes."

"You've had no letters or postcards from her that might indicate her whereabouts?" he asked suspiciously.

"Angie seldom wrote—no, I've had no communication from abroad." I waited, almost holding my breath, for him to ask if I'd ever had a letter from her, but he sighed and turned to Tom.

"When did you last see Mrs. Blauvelt, Doctor?"

Tom explained that he'd never met Angie and had spoken to her only once on the telephone years ago when I was in the hospital. The lieutenant then asked where he'd been on Friday last, the day of the murder. After making a list of the patients Tom had seen, he turned to me and asked how I had spent the day. I thought I saw a flash of interest, possibly surprise, when I said I worked in a bookstore and had been there from nine to five except for the hour between one and two when I came home for lunch. He took down the address of the store and then stood up, putting the notebook back in his pocket.

"You're quite sure Mrs. Blauvelt is abroad?" he asked, looking from one to the other of us. "You see, we found a monogrammed handkerchief on the floor, next to where Mr. Blauvelt lay on the couch. The initials are AEB. If you hear from Angela Evans Blauvelt, or find out where she is, please get in touch with me. I can be reached at this number."

He nodded to us, then took his leave.

Tom and I were both stunned by the lieutenant's revelation concerning Angie's handkerchief, and the only explanation we could offer for its presence next to the dead man was not a particularly convincing one. Derek, we postulated, might have found it among Angie's things and detecting the scent she used, held it up to his face while he thought about her. By his own admission, he still longed for her at times. . . .

We stayed up late that night, talking about Derek—how Angie had met him, how he had courted her, and how he had changed from the cold, unbending person who had at first frightened Kitty and Megan to the kindly, avuncular man we had come to know.

"I'm reminded of Scrooge, and the change in him," I said,

"except that Scrooge found happiness in the end, something poor Derek never found—unless it was in the early days of his marriage."

"I know what you mean, honey," Tom said, "and I agree with you up to a point, but I think Derek was far more flawed and complicated than Scrooge, who was essentially a selfish old man obsessed with money. Derek seemed torn between two obsessions—his compelling desire to keep up appearances at any cost and his almost uncontrollable love—or lust—for Angie. And there were definitely two sides to Derek's nature—the warm, generous one you and the children know and the angry one that surfaced the night he heard Angie had been in a brothel. I'm not saying he was a Jekyll and Hyde, but he was without a doubt two-sided. Ah well. He's gone now. . . ."

I did not sleep well that night, even with Tom's body curved comfortingly around mine.

Because of the manner of Derek's death, the executors of his will delayed probating it and notifying his beneficiaries, so it was not until a few days before Thanksgiving that I learned he had set up trust funds for Kitty, Megan, and me. There were several other bequests, but the bulk of his fortune went to a number of charitable organizations he had supported during his lifetime, and Blauvelt House was to be converted into a home for destitute women. Was that his way of making some sort of provision for Angie, since he had not named her in his will? I knew, though, that she'd never go there, even as a last resort.

We heard nothing further from Lieutenant Moran, and gradually the newspapers dropped all mention of the murder. I began to think the police had given up their investigation, but Tom said they'd keep the case open for years if necessary; open, but unsolved. I had a mental picture of a file with

Derek's name on it gathering dust in some little-used room, waiting, waiting for his assailant to be brought to justice, so that someone in authority could write CASE CLOSED on the cover and Derek's uneasy spirit might be laid to rest.

I know now, though, that the truth of the matter will never be made public.

XXI

In December we found a house that pleased us. I could not repress a smile when I thought of how my father would have approved of our moving "west" to Thirty-eighth Street between Madison and Fifth Avenues where the "nobs" lived. We also found that I was pregnant, and Tom insisted that I give up the bookstore as soon as Mr. Heimlich could replace me.

"No one could 'replace' you, Maud," the bookseller said regretfully. "Oh, I'll find another typewriter, but it won't be the same at all. Not many people bring light and grace into a room the way you do. And Danny will be sore wroth. . . ."

He hired another young woman a few days later. After I spent a morning with her showing her what to do, I left, promising to drop in from time to time to see him and to check on the progress of the opus. (I did do that too, and about two years later Danny sent me an autographed copy of *Solitary Cliffs,* which reviewers hailed as a brilliant first novel.)

I walked home slowly that day, sorry in a way that the pleasant daily association I'd had with Mr. Heimlich and Danny was over but glad that I'd be able to give my full attention to the coming move.

The house we purchased suited us both. Tom liked it because the former owner, a physician, had installed a separate entrance to his office at street level next to the high stoop that led up to the family quarters. "Makes it easier for the halt and the lame to get in," he said when we were being shown through the property.

The rooms on the floor above, all of which opened off a central hall, delighted me, with the parlor and dining room on one side, and sitting room, study, and kitchen on the other. The three upper floors were given over to bedrooms, although I thought I'd use one of them for what used to be called a morning room.

The other houses we'd looked at, like the majority of New York brownstones, had windows only in the front and the rear, which resulted in gloom and darkness in the interior rooms. In our case, an alley about six or eight feet wide ran between our house and the one next to it, allowing daylight to stream through the windows of the rooms facing west. And it would be *my* house, without anything in it to remind me of the past.

As I had once said to Tom, I had no particular feeling for the house I had lived in for the greater part of my life, but on the afternoon of Christmas Eve, as I sat by the fire, I couldn't help but feel slightly nostalgic. I could hear Kitty and Megan laughing and talking in the kitchen as they helped Kathleen decorate Christmas cookies and was reminded of Angie at that age doing the same thing, with Mama bustling about, supervising everything. It was a fleeting memory and a pleasant one, but I didn't dwell on it. It seemed that all the happiness of holidays before the boat trip had been washed away that dreadful day on the East River. No, I told myself, I was relieved that this would be our last Christmas on Thirty-second Street, and to prevent my mind from lingering on the past, I picked up the copy of the latest Rinehart mystery that Mr. Heimlich had pressed on me, but I hadn't read more than a few pages when the phone rang.

My heart seemed to stand still for a moment when I recognized the voice. "Angie! Angie! Is that you?"

"None other, Maudie dear. Merry Christmas and all that!"

"Where are you? Will you come—"

"No, I can't. We're about to leave for England. I'll write to you from there."

I could hear a male voice in the background, but the words were indistinguishable.

"Angie, couldn't I see you before you go? Just for a little—"

"I'm afraid not, Maudie. We're on our way to the boat."

"Who's going with you? Have you married again? You know about Derek, don't you?"

Instead of answering me, she laughed and said Merry Christmas again. Then the line went dead.

"She must be all right, honey," Tom said when I told him about the phone call. "People don't sail for England unless they're pretty well off. Let me see the paper—yes, here it is. The *Berengaria* is due to sail tonight at eight. What time did she call?"

"About five, I think. She sounded happy enough, but strange—I wondered if she'd been drinking. And she wouldn't answer my questions. She just laughed and hung up. I thought I heard a man's voice. Maybe she couldn't speak freely."

"That's probably it, honey. And you said she sounded happy—that's what counts. In any case, she said she'd write to you, didn't she?"

"Yes, but I doubt that she will. I know Angie."

Neither of us thought of calling Lieutenant Moran—at least I didn't, and if Tom did, he didn't mention it.

To my surprise, Angie did write. The letter reached me when we were still settling into the new house. Ellen Grady, who came to us when Kathleen married her Patrick the day after Christmas, brought it to me with the rest of the mail one cold, sleety afternoon in February. It had been forwarded from the Thirty-second Street house and bore no return address, just a London postmark.

January 4, 1911

Dear Maudie,

Surprise! You thought I'd never write, didn't you? Just wanted to let you know that I'm finally settled; I know what a worrier you are. I'm married too, to a splendid man (nothing like Derek), and have all that a woman could want.

A word of warning: If that nasty Mrs. Williams (remember the housekeeper?) comes to you wanting to know where I am, DON'T TELL HER! She's after some money I borrowed (I wouldn't want Edgar to know about that). I had to cross the ocean to get away from her (and a few others), but I'm safe and happy now.

Love,

Angie

XXII

Just like Angie, I thought as I sat holding the letter and remembering how she had never told me any more than she wanted me to know. I was surprised that she admitted to owing Mrs. Williams money but not at all surprised that she didn't want her new husband to know about it. It was rather dismaying, too, to read that there were "a few others" she wanted to avoid. Was she in debt to them as well?

I was consoling myself with the thought that at least she was happily married, and far away from Blauvelt House and all that had happened under its roof when Tom came up from the office.

"Two patients canceled their appointments," he said after kissing me and pulling his chair closer to the fire. "And I can't say I blame them. The streets are so icy that I sent Miss Tierney home early. Did the girls get in from school? Ah, here they are. Did you two slide all the way home?"

"Not all the way," Megan answered. "Ellen made us hold onto the railings."

"That I did, Doctor," Ellen said, coming in with the tea tray. "I didn't want any broken bones, theirs or mine."

"Good for you, Ellen." Tom smiled as he watched her arrange the cups on the table near me. "Now I want to hear about the spelling bee, Kitty. Did you remember the *i*-before-*e* rule?"

I sat back comfortably in the rocking chair Tom had bought for me and half-listened to the enthusiastic chatter of the two girls while I continued to think about Angie's letter. I wondered if Tom would say we ought to show it to Lieutenant Moran, and later on, when we were alone in the sitting room after dinner, I brought the subject up.

"I suppose we should have told Lieutenant Moran about her phone call on Christmas Eve," I said, "but I didn't think of it at the time. I guess I really hated the thought of his going after her—oh, Tom, do you think I'll spend the rest of my life covering up for Angie? Keeping quiet about things I know?"

"No, I don't honey. She's—" The ringing of the front doorbell interrupted him, and he went to answer it, muttering something about who would be fool enough to be out in such weather. When he returned to the sitting room a few minutes later, I saw with a start that he was accompanied by the man whose name I had just mentioned. And Angie's letter lay in full view on the table where Tom had dropped it.

"Mrs. Cavanaugh, I do apologize for barging in on you," the detective said in his quiet, cultured voice, "but I couldn't get through on the telephone—ice on the wires, I imagine—and I wanted to tell you the news before you read it in the morning papers. I think it will interest you."

"It's quite all right, Lieutenant," I said, making an effort to hide my nervousness. "Won't you sit down?"

"Thank you. I'll tell you at once, then, that Mr. Blauvelt's murderer—or rather, murderess—has been found and that your sister, wherever she is, is in the clear. She's been on my mind."

"Murderess?" I murmured stupidly.

"Yes. A Mrs. Cora Williams. We have the evidence at last. We've suspected her for some time, but like your sister, she disappeared, and it has taken us a while to locate her."

I was so relieved that Angie was innocent that I had to force myself to concentrate on what he was saying.

"I was never satisfied," he said, leaning forward in the chair and looking from me to Tom, "that in a mansion with a fairly large staff such as the one in Blauvelt House, no one, absolutely no one, had seen a sign of a stranger—or, in this case, a known person—in the house or on the grounds in the middle of the afternoon. And I was right to be dissatisfied. With the exception of the caretaker and his wife, all the help has been let go, but we were able to find and question every one of them again—the maids, the cook, the housekeeper, the gardeners—everyone. It was one of the maids who broke the case for us. Do you remember a small timid-looking little woman named Effie Macklin? Yes. Well, she saw enough to put Mrs. Williams behind bars for twenty years to life if it's second-degree murder, or in the electric chair if it's murder in the first degree."

"Why did Effie Macklin wait so long to come forward?" Tom asked.

"Sheer terror," the detective responded. "She lived in mortal fear of Mrs. Williams when she was a housekeeper, a fear that persisted—"

"Yes," I said. "I remember seeing Effie turn pale whenever Mrs. Williams appeared. And the children saw the house-keeper abusing the poor thing physically."

"I am not surprised," Lieutenant Moran said, nodding his head, "although Effie said nothing about that. I had a feeling she was hiding something—it's a certain look people get, a look I've learned to spot—but after we convinced her that no harm would come to her, she talked.

"It seems that she was taking her afternoon rest on a chair

she'd pulled into the shade behind some hydrangea bushes near a gazebo where she couldn't be seen from the house. She said she thought she was almost asleep when a squirrel jumped down from the roof to the gazebo and startled her. Then, out of the corner of her eye, she saw a movement in the shrubbery near the terrace outside the study, and a moment later the Williams woman came into view. One of the French doors was ajar, and Effie saw Mrs. Williams open it wider and enter the house.

"At that point, Effie said, she 'went cold all over' for fear the woman had seen her in one of the master's garden chairs, forgetting completely that Mrs. Williams was no longer the housekeeper. She told us that the very sight of that figure dressed in black was enough to 'drive her witless'—her words. She stayed where she was, and a few minutes later she saw Mrs. Williams come out of the house and disappear behind the shrubbery. Effie did not see her again, and it's easy enough to understand why. The dense greenery—rhododendrons, laurel, and the like—provide an effective screen for anyone making for the woods that border the property. And that's where we think Williams went.

"Effie waited—she's not sure how long—until she had screwed up enough courage to run as fast as she could to the back of the house and into the servants' wing. At first she thought she'd lock herself in her room and stay there for the rest of the day, but she knew that would be impossible. It was her duty to take Mr. Blauvelt's tea in to him every afternoon, so at four o'clock, as usual, she carried the tray down the hall to the study.

"She knocked on the door and opened it without waiting for an answer. She thought it a bit unusual that Mr. Blauvelt was lying on the couch at that hour—she didn't look at him closely, but assumed he was asleep—and decided to leave the tray for him. So it wasn't until half an hour later, when she went to collect the tea things, that the alarm was given, and by that time, Mrs. Williams was well away.'' He paused for a moment and cleared his throat.

"Would you care for a drink, Lieutenant? Scotch?'' Tom asked.

"Thanks, but I'd better not. Another time maybe.''

"How did you find her? Effie, I mean,'' I asked.

"Oh, that was simple. James, the caretaker, told us that Mrs. Van Tieck, who replaced Williams as housekeeper, had taken her along with her when she found a position in Irvington. I thought you were going to ask how we found Mrs. Williams. That was not so simple. It took a while. As you may know, we have connections with police all over the country, and she was finally located in Eastport, out on Long Island. God knows why she went there. If she'd wanted to hide out, she'd have had a better chance right here in New York. But that's beside the point. She was living in a small, rather shabby frame house with her brother, Robert Orkney. He's a big brute and apparently not too sharp. I gathered he was dependent on her for his livelihood, but he had no more love for her than Effie had. He was more than ready to cooperate with us, to get even with her for making his life miserable. He sat with a satisfied smile on his face when we charged her with the murder of Mr. Blauvelt and watched, still smiling, when she flew into a rage—a terrible rage. I would call it maniacal.

"She must have been afraid Robert would tell what he knew because before we could stop her, she pulled a carving knife out of a drawer and went for him, screaming obscenities. It was not a pretty sight, and my sergeant and I had all we could do to restrain her. She fought like a she-wolf—she's a strong woman—biting, kicking, flailing her arms around, and in the end drooling at the mouth. Finally she slumped in the chair we had tied her up in and grunted—the weirdest noise I ever heard a human make. I'm wondering now if she'll be fit to stand trial. If not, she'll be sent to the prison for the criminally insane."

"What about Effie, Lieutenant?" I asked. "Will she have to testify?"

"If it comes to a trial, yes."

"Will Effie's testimony stand up in court?" Tom asked. "It seems—"

"Unsubstantial? By itself, yes, it is. But as I said earlier, we have other evidence. In Mr. Blauvelt's safe we found a number of anonymous letters, each of which demanded that he send certain large amounts of money, in cash, to a box at the General Post Office here in the city or risk exposure."

"Derek risk exposure!" I gasped at the thought. "What on earth could he have done?"

"We don't know that yet, Mrs. Cavanaugh. We may never know, but she obviously knew something to his discredit that he did not want revealed. His bank statements show that the amounts he withdrew in cash at stated intervals correspond to the amounts requested in the blackmail letters. Mrs. Williams made an effort to disguise her handwriting, but our experts have proved that it is indeed hers. And we found most of the money, over thirty thousand dollars, hidden under a floorboard in the attic of the Eastport house.

"To go on—and this ties it up for us—a week before Mr. Blauvelt's death last August, Mrs. Williams received a letter from him stating that she could expect no further payments. It was sent to the post-office box and contained no money. She took it home with her, intending to answer it, I suppose, with further threats, but who knows what she had in mind? In any case, she tore up Mr. Blauvelt's letter and threw it in the trash. But the brother, Robert, who had heard her swearing when she reread the letter, got hold of it and pieced it together.

"He said she hardly spoke for the next few days, except to mutter threats against Mr. Blauvelt. Then, on the twenty-seventh of August, the day he was killed, she took the train to the city and did not return until after dark. Robert didn't think anything of it—she'd been traveling into New York regularly to pick up the mail at the General Post Office—until he read about the murder in the newspaper. Then he was frightened. He was even more frightened when he showed her the headlines and all she did was laugh and tell him to mind his own business.

" 'She always told me what to do,' he said. 'She and my other sister, Pauline. Pauline wasn't so bad. I didn't mind working for her, but she went and died, and then Cora came,' " Lieutenant Moran read from the notebook to which he had been referring from time to time.

"Robert isn't retarded, but he is slow-witted, and Mrs. Williams had him completely under her thumb. He told us a somewhat garbled story about how she made him go with her one night the summer before last to help her break into Blauvelt House—"

"I was there!" I cried. "So it was she! Derek was in New York that night—she must have known that—and nobody heard anything because of a dreadful thunderstorm."

"Yes. Robert mentioned a storm and said he was hoping his sister would be struck by lightning. She made him break a pane of glass and open the French door. Then he had to stand watch while she tried to find the key to the safe. Robert was a bit vague, but he didn't think she succeeded. It was after that, early in September, that she started writing the anonymous letters. Yes, Mrs. Cavanaugh?"

"It was a few days after the break-in that she came to see Derek. She drove up in a taxi. Was she blackmailing him then, do you think? He never mentioned her visit, although he must have known I was aware of it."

"Without a doubt, blackmail was her purpose, but when he

wouldn't cooperate anymore, she was determined to make him pay, one way or another," the lieutenant answered.

"What will happen to Robert? Will he go to trial?" Tom asked.

"Probably. We're holding him while the case against him is being built up. Failure to report his suspicions to the police, criminal trespass, accomplice in the break-in, et cetera. It's hard to say right now what the outcome will be."

He glanced down at his notebook, then looked up at us. "Oh, yes," he said with a trace of a smile. "One last item. In a box in one of Mrs. Williams's chests we found a pile of lace-trimmed handkerchiefs with your sister's monogram on them. Obviously Mrs. Williams had stolen them from Blauvelt House before she left there, and just as obviously, she dropped one in the study to cast suspicion on Mrs. Blauvelt—a transparent attempt . . ."

Lieutenant Moran sighed and heaved himself out of the easy chair. "I must go," he said in a tired voice, "and let you get to bed. I came mainly on account of Mrs. Blauvelt. I saw her once at a charity ball given to raise money for the Policemen's Pension Fund. She was the most beautiful creature I'd ever seen."

He left then, without so much as a glance at the letter lying on the end table next to Tom's chair.

As Lieutenant Moran had suspected, Mrs. Williams was declared unfit to stand trial; she was committed to an asylum for the insane where she died of self-starvation within a short time. Robert was prosecuted for his part in Derek's murder, but the defense attorney was able to convince the jury that he had been an "unwilling" accomplice and that he was mentally incapable of disobeying his strong-minded sister. He was sentenced to three years' probation, and according to Lieutenant Moran, continued to live in the small house in Eastport, supporting himself by doing odd jobs for the duck farmers in the area. The blackmail money, more than thirty thousand dollars, reverted to Derek's estate.

I had no interest in Robert, but when I heard that Mrs. Williams had died, the thought that sprang to my mind was that it would be safe now for Angie to come home—but I had no way of letting her know.

XXIII

As things turned out, there was no need for me to tell Angie anything. Shortly after the death of Mrs. Williams I received a jubilant letter from London, this time with a return address (because of Derek's prominence in international finance, the British newspapers had carried stories of the solving of his murder and the subsequent death of the housekeeper):

> *I can come and see you now, and I will one of these days.*
> *I can't tell you how relieved I am! Everything is fine here.*
> *We live quietly—neither of us cares to go out in society—*
> *but we do manage a couple of weeks in Scotland each year,*
> *so that Edgar can fish for salmon. It's a marvelous part of*
> *the world; you'd love it, Maudie.*
>
> *Give my love to the "little ones," although I guess*
> *they're not so little now.*
>
> *Love,*
> *Angie*

I answered her letter immediately, inviting her and Edgar to visit us as soon as possible, but it wasn't until the fall of

1914 that she came. England was at war, and Edgar, who was likely to be called up, thought she'd be safer in New York than in London.

By that time our little boy, Tommy, was two and a half and very much the center of attention in the household. Kitty and Megan waited on him hand and foot, played with him, fed him, and even took turns bathing him under the supervision of his nurse. The afternoon Angie arrived, they were with me in the sitting room trying to teach Tommy to sing the alphabet, when I saw her taxi draw up.

At first glance I thought she looked painfully thin, but later, when I saw her delighted smile at the warmth of her welcome (even Tommy rose to the occasion by presenting her with his toy elephant) and heard her talking like the old Angie, I forgot about my initial impression until I was alone with Tom that evening in our bedroom.

"Has Angie said anything about not feeling well, honey?" he asked as he unbuttoned his shirt. "She only picked at her food at dinner, and she doesn't look—"

"She just said she was terribly tired, Tom. The crossing was a bad one. It took two weeks because of the way the ship had to zigzag to avoid the German submarines. And the weather was stormy, too. She was seasick for most of the trip, she said."

"That's probably all it is, then," he said. "Feed her up, honey, and see that she gets plenty of rest."

That wasn't all it was, though. Although Angie went to bed early and slept late, the fatigue persisted. I noticed that even the slight exertion involved in walking to the corner to mail a letter to Edgar taxed her strength. She wasn't eating well, either. When I tried to coax her to take more than one of the tiny sandwiches Cook sent up with our afternoon tea, she just shook her head.

"When my appetite returns, Maudie," she said with a little

smile, "I'll eat you out of house and home, but I don't think I'm completely over the mal de mer yet."

I decided to wait until she felt better before asking any questions about Mrs. Williams, Derek, Blauvelt House, or where she'd been before she fled to England, and Angie seemed to want to think about the future instead of dwelling on the past. She and Edgar were planning to buy a cottage in Cornwall for a weekend retreat, she said, but of course not until the war ended. Her eyes lit up when she described one they had already seen, a real storybook cottage, according to her. She talked a good deal about their life in London; so much, in fact, that I had the feeling that she was making a deliberate effort to avoid any reference to our former lives.

She'd been with us for almost a week when I came upon her in the parlor one afternoon sitting with her eyes closed and looking so pale and drawn that I was frightened. "Angie, don't you think you should let Tom look you over?" I asked. "Maybe a tonic—"

"Oh, Maudie, what a worrier you are!" she said impatiently. "You haven't changed a bit in that respect, but I must say you've grown prettier with the years. Marriage agrees with you, obviously. No, I don't need a tonic. I'm fine. You pamper me so—and I love it!"

I knew it would be useless to try to persuade her to change her mind—she would simply put me off—so I let it go. But when she collapsed at the dinner table the following night, there was no need for persuasion. She was in no condition to protest.

Tom acted swiftly, and before Angie realized what was happening, he'd had her admitted to Bellevue for observation and tests. He called me the next day at noon to say that she'd had emergency surgery for acute appendicitis and was not yet out of danger.

"She's asked for you several times, honey, so perhaps you'd

better drop in later this afternoon. Don't be shocked when you see her. She's been through a lot and is still not out of the woods. There was a walled abscess on the appendix, which had ruptured. If she'd come to us sooner, we might have been able to keep the infection from spreading. Look, honey, don't stay too long. She's pretty weak."

In spite of his warning, I nearly cried out when I saw how white and fragile she looked lying in the high hospital bed with her eyes closed.

"Angie," I said softly, hoping I would be able to hold back the tears that threatened.

"Maudie, oh, Maudie," she whispered. "I've needed you. I need to tell you . . . but I'm so tired . . . hold my hand."

She closed her eyes again, and drifted off to sleep as I sat watching her, holding her thin fingers in mine. When it seemed that she was deeply asleep, I removed my hand gently and wrote a note saying I'd be back the next day. I laid it on the little table next to the bed and slipped out of the room, no longer able to keep from crying.

I was standing in the corridor, sniffling and searching for a handkerchief, when Tom put his arm around my shoulders and guided me into a small office.

"She's dying, isn't she, Tom?" I asked when I could speak. "What—"

"We're not sure yet, honey," he said slowly. "If we can control the infection, she'll pull through, but—"

"If not, how long . . ?"

"It's hard to say, honey. A month—maybe a little longer. I think you should let Edgar know how serious it is. In the meantime, there's further treatment scheduled for tomorrow morning."

"I'll come in the afternoon, then. I left a note for her saying I'd be back tomorrow. I can leave as soon as Tommy goes down for his nap. It's Nurse Whitlow's afternoon off, but Ellen can manage."

For the next several weeks all my afternoons were devoted to Angie. The time I spent with her each day varied, depending on whether she was in pain and had been sedated or was awake and fairly comfortable. Some days she'd be sitting up in the chair near the window, but usually she was lying quietly in bed.

At first she asked a few, very few, questions about Tommy and the girls, but it was obvious that she was anxious to talk about herself. Over the course of those weeks she told me, not always in chronological order, what had happened to her after she ran away from Derek.

Of course, I was already familiar with parts of her story, but a great deal of it was new to me and served to fill in gaps that Tom and I had wondered about. I was so nervous and upset at that time that I was afraid I might forget some of the things she said, so each night, beginning October 20, 1914, I wrote down (in her own words insofar as I could remember them) what she told me. Somehow it seemed important that there be a record of Angie's life.

Oct. 20. Maudie, I've been thinking: Do you realize that we, you and I, had to become adults almost overnight when Mama and the twins and Johnnie were killed? We weren't exactly children when the *Slocum* went down, but nothing in our lives until then had prepared us for what came afterward. And we had no one to guide us. I think I'm trying to excuse myself— oh, maybe I should tell a priest what happened—but I don't want to talk to a stranger. And I *can't* tell Edgar—he's coming, isn't he? You're the only one I can tell, and maybe then you'll understand it all and why I had to stay away so long.

I'd still be in England if it hadn't been for the war. I really was happy there. But Edgar was so worried. He had to pull all kinds of strings to get me on that boat.

Speaking of boats, I don't know why I keep staring at the river, watching the ships go by, when I hate it so much! It ruined my whole life! You remember what things were like before Mama died, don't you? And what Papa was like afterward? And *you* know I pushed him. You saw it all, but you never said anything. Were you as relieved as I that he was dead? Oh, that doesn't matter—I did it. You didn't.

Oct. 21. I don't want to talk about Derek, but I have to. I was a fool to marry him, but I had no idea what it would be like to marry a man I didn't love. How could I have known? All I could think of was money, and he had plenty of that. I was desperate, for fear you and Megan and Kitty and I would end up paupers. I couldn't have stood that, so I accepted the first rich man who came my way. He gave me everything I asked for, but believe me, I paid for it.

He regulated my whole life, almost every hour of the day. I was told which charity board meeting to go to, which invitations to accept and which to decline, all that. It was boring, but I probably could have put up with that part. It was the other thing that drove me away from him and made me hate him. You see, he was insistent, almost insatiable sexually, and I simply dreaded and despised his lovemaking! His pasty complexion, his sour breath, and his bandy legs turned my stomach every time! He wanted me every night, too. Oh, I don't want to think about it.

I suppose you're wondering why we never had a child? I'm not positive, but I think it was because he had had the mumps when he was a boy, and thank God he did! I'd have had a baby every year otherwise, and I never wanted children. That didn't stop him, though, from demanding his "rights," and I found out later that when I didn't oblige, he'd go to someone else for satisfaction.

Do you remember that summer at Blauvelt House, how he used to go to New York or Washington for a couple of days at a time? He said it was on business, and I'm sure he did have things to attend to in the office, or with people in Washington—remember how close he was to Teddy Roosevelt? But his nights were not spent at the office, and they weren't spent alone. I know. I'll tell you later how I found out.

Oct. 22. (Angie was asleep when I went to the hospital today, so I didn't stay.)

Oct. 23. I was talking about Derek, wasn't I, Maudie? Remember how he kept me a prisoner that summer? Well, even while you were still there, I'd started thinking about getting away. I knew I'd need money, and I didn't want to steal, even though I knew he kept quite a bit of cash in the safe in the study. I couldn't have gotten at that anyway. So I waited. . . .

You see, he kept me there because he'd found out that I'd been seeing Gregory Ellis, a man quite different from himself, a man who taught me how wonderful love can be and made me feel like a beloved, cherished woman, not just an outlet for passion. And he was young! I wanted more than anything to be with him, to have him hold me in his arms, and Derek must have sensed that. In the end, strangely enough, it was Mrs. Williams who made it possible for me to go to Gregory.

I thought Derek had set the housekeeper to watch me (I told you that, didn't I, that morning in the gazebo?), and one day when he was away—this was after you'd gone back to the city—I accused her of spying on me. She denied it, of course, but when I threatened to complain to Derek about her, a sly look came over her face.

"It won't do you any good, madam," she said. "And you

shouldn't be so quick to judge me. I may yet be of service to you.''

I had no idea what she meant——oh, it will take too long to tell you now, Maudie, and I have such a pain. Come back tomorrow.

Oct. 24. I found out what Mrs. Williams meant by being ''of service'' to me almost a week later when Derek was away. She knocked on my bedroom door that evening and asked if I could spare her a few minutes. Before I could answer, she came in and sat down in a chair opposite mine in front of the fire I had lighted earlier. The rain was beating against the windows, and when the lamps flickered, I suddenly felt uncomfortable. I should have said right then that I was sleepy and wanted to go to bed, but I didn't. It was as if she had hypnotized me with those dark eyes of hers, and I said nothing.

Finally she made her proposition. ''I do not like to see anyone miserable, my dear,'' she said with an attempt at a smile, ''and it is obvious that you are not a happy woman. With your beauty, you could go far——''

I started to say something. I don't remember what it was, but she held up her hand and interrupted me. ''Let me go on. I know a great deal about human nature. I've been observing it for a number of years, and I have a good idea about what is going on in your mind. You would be a great asset in a business in which I have an interest, my dear. You could make a lot of money. And I want you to know that I am in a position to help——''

''I don't need your help!'' I shouted. ''Please be good enough to leave my room. At once!''

She rose slowly from the chair and just as slowly walked to the door where she turned and looked at me knowingly. ''You *will* need it, Mrs. Blauvelt,'' she said softly. Then she left.

I locked my door that night, but even so, I lay awake for hours and hours.

When Derek came back, I asked him to dismiss Mrs. Williams, saying I found her presence distasteful. He refused point-blank. His mother had hired her years ago, he said, and he had no intention of letting her go. I wondered then how old the housekeeper was. Her face was unlined, her hair still coal-black, and yet she couldn't have been young. She could have passed for thirty, I suppose, but I thought she must be nearer fifty—don't ask me why.

I wasn't lying to Derek when I said she made me uncomfortable. She did. In fact, she almost frightened me. Why on earth would she dare intrude on my privacy? I couldn't imagine what her game was. If Derek had told her to spy on me, then why did she offer to help me? And was his real reason for keeping her that he needed her to watch me? Or was there something I didn't know?

She didn't bother me again for a while, not until one night when she saw me going up the stairs in tears after Derek and I had had an argument.

(At this point Angie turned her head away from me and stopped talking. She lay still, not responding to my questions or remarks. A little later a nurse came in and glancing at her patient, signaled to me that it was time to leave. The next day, Angie went right on with her story in a hurried sort of way, as if she were afraid she wouldn't have time to finish it.)

Oct. 25. I was telling you about the night of the argument, wasn't I? Well, I wanted to go back to New York, to the house on Fifth Avenue, but Derek wouldn't consider it. I was utterly miserable, almost frantic, at the thought of the days, weeks, even months alone in that isolated mansion. I imagine that if I hadn't been feeling so upset, I would have been more on my guard—but who knows? As I said, Mrs. Williams saw me crying and picked that moment to tempt me.

She followed me into my room, closing the door behind her. She began by saying that if I continued with the life I was leading, I would go mad, and I thought maybe she was right.

"I've seen such things happen, my dear," she went on when I remained silent. "A beautiful girl like you isn't cut out for loneliness. Now listen to me. I have a plan."

I forget her exact words, but what it amounted to was this: Derek was to leave for Washington in the morning and would be gone for three days, so there would be nothing to stop me from running away. She would give me some money and the address of a flat in New York where I would be safe, and free of his attentions. (How could she have known about that part?) Then I could get on with my life. Later on, she would find employment, pleasant employment, for me. I foolishly told her I had tried to leave him once before—Maudie, you remember that—and how he came for me at Thirty-second Street—but Mrs. Williams said he'd never find me if I did what she told me. Of course, I had no idea then what she was planning for me.

I knew I oughtn't to trust her, and I did hold off until the day before Derek's return. I knew he would insist on making love to me the next night and I knew I simply couldn't bear it. Also, the thought of being free of him, and seeing Gregory again, was the first happy thought I'd had in months and months. Well, the temptation was too much for me to resist any longer. . . . Maudie, call the nurse, will you?

Oct. 26. (I was told Angie had had a bad night and that it would be better if I didn't see her.)

Oct. 27. I had a little setback, Maudie, but I'm better today. Where was I? Oh yes—I left Blauvelt House that night for good. I took only a few clothes with me and the jewelry I was wearing, and when Mrs. Williams smuggled me out of the house and into a cab she had waiting down the road, she gave me an envelope full of money. I remember wondering how she happened to have so much cash—five thousand dollars—and when I exclaimed about it, she said that it was nothing, that I'd be earning far more than that in no time. I didn't want to think about earning money. I was too excited and nervous, too anxious to see Gregory, to worry about that then.

I had no trouble finding the flat, which turned out to be a rather nice one on the Upper West Side, and everything was fine until the landlady (a friend of Mrs. Williams's, of course) objected when Gregory stayed overnight. He suggested that I move in with him, so I waited until I saw the woman go out one morning and then I slipped out myself, thinking that once and for all I'd be free of Mrs. Williams as well as of Derek. Gregory lived down below Washington Square in a nice enough place, just two rooms and a studio. Did I tell you he was an artist? I'd met him the year before at a soirée the Rhinelanders gave to celebrate the opening of a new art gallery.

It wasn't gracious living, by any means, but I'd had enough of that, and we were absurdly happy. I adored Gregory—oh, Maudie, he was wonderful! Thoughtful, handsome, tender, and *young!* Only two years older than I. Being with him was sheer delight, and we didn't worry about a thing—at least until the money ran out.

It's amazing how fast even five thousand dwindles away, and Gregory hadn't sold a picture for some time. I didn't mind being poor with him. It's different when you're in love. But when we could no longer pay the rent, I didn't know what to do. Finally I decided to go up to Thirty-second Street and ask you for a loan. I thought you'd have some money, because I never really believed Derek would stop supporting you because I left him. You know how he felt about charity—it was a sacred duty to him, as it had been to his parents.

Well, by that time it was July, and when I saw that the house was all closed up, I was pretty sure that Derek had taken you to Tarrytown again. I couldn't think of any place else you might be. I still had my key—thank goodness I'd kept it—and Gregory and I moved in. I found the money you'd left in the shoe box, and I really meant to put it back, but we were always so short. Gregory earned a little from time to time painting signs, enough to keep us in food, but that's about all. My, it seemed funny to be cooking in that old kitchen again! I stayed in most of the time, afraid that I might run into Derek.

Oct. 28. (Another bad day. I was not allowed to see her.)

Oct. 29. So we stayed in the house for the summer. We talked about what to do in the fall when you would be back. I knew you wouldn't put us out, Maudie, but I was certain that Derek would find me if we stayed. So toward the end of August we moved into a single room on Twentieth Street, and that's where Mrs. Williams caught up with me.

If we'd only gone to another part of the city, things would have been different, but of course I had no idea then that she was in New York. How could I? If I thought about her at all, I pictured her prowling through the halls of Blauvelt House. Anyway, Gregory had an artist friend, Henry Cope, who lived in the house we moved into, where the room was cheap and clean. An added attraction was that Gregory could share Henry's studio on the floor above us. It really was quite pleasant—for a while.

We'd been there a couple of months when it happened. I was standing in front of the butcher's shop thinking I'd go in and buy a cheap cut of meat to make a stew for our dinner (I didn't have much money, naturally) when I turned and saw her. I started to move away, but she caught my arm and held on to me. I tried to shrug her off, but I couldn't. She had a grip like a man's, and she wouldn't let me go.

"You owe me something, don't you?" she asked. "Five thousand dollars, as I remember."

I said yes, I did remember and that I'd pay her back as soon as I could. Then she turned all sweet and pleasant and asked me to have a cup of tea with her so we could talk things over comfortably. She was visiting her sister, who had a house on Twenty-first Street, she said. I tried to refuse, saying that it was getting late and that I had dinner to prepare, but she said she knew how I could repay her and that we simply had to talk about it. In the end I went with her.

Oh, Maudie, I don't know where my wits were! Papa used to say I had the looks but you had the brains. I think he was right, although you seem to have both now. You're really quite lovely, you know.

But to go on. I was surprised to see that Mrs. Williams's sister had a doorman, a large surly fellow, who let us in, and I was more surprised when he locked and bolted the door behind us as soon as we were inside. She ushered me into a parlor, a garish, overfurnished room, all satin and brocade, and rang for tea.

While we were waiting for it to arrive, she took a slip of paper from the desk in the corner of the room and held it up in front of me, but not close enough so that I could read what it said. "See, my dear," she said, smiling, "this is the note you signed promising to repay the money you borrowed from me at the end of six months, plus interest."

I protested that I had never signed a note, but she maintained that I had, just before I left Blauvelt House. I knew I hadn't done any such thing, but I could not deny that I owed her the money. First she terrified me with threats of arrest and prison, and then her manner changed, and she suggested that I work for her.

We were silent while the maid brought in the tea, which Mrs. Williams poured, remarking with a smirk that she remembered that I liked both sugar and milk in mine, while she took hers plain. The tea warmed me, and as I drank it, I looked around the room wondering what more she had to say. Perhaps, I thought, I might make a few dollars working for her, but doing what? Of all the crazy thoughts . . .

"You will have extremely pleasant duties," she said, as if she'd read my thoughts, "and with your looks, you'll be a great success."

She was staring at me, and all at once I had trouble focusing my eyes. The last thing I remember hearing was her telling someone to carry me upstairs. The tea must have had a drug in it, or maybe it was in the sugar she added. Anyway—oh, Maudie, I'm tired now. I've been talking too much.

Oct. 30. When I woke up, she told me I had fainted and must rest. She would take care of me, she said, and see that I had proper food. I must have slept again, and when I woke up the second time, my mind was clear. Gregory would be worried, I thought. I got up from the bed and tried to open the door. When I realized it was locked and remembered the locks and bolts on the front door, the thought flashed through my mind that I had exchanged the prison of Blauvelt House for a prison on Twenty-first Street. I began to scream to be let out, and after a few minutes Mrs. Williams came in and told me to be quiet. What a liar that woman was! When I said I had to leave at once, she insisted that I had agreed to work for her (which I hadn't, of course) and that I would have to stay until I had earned enough to repay what I owed. In the meantime, I was not to try to escape. The windows were barred, the doors guarded.

"Very well guarded," she said, "and Robert is incorruptible. In the meantime, my dear, why don't you just relax in this very comfortable room. I take pride in providing excellent living accommodations for my guests. I will have your food brought to you, and when you feel rested, you can amuse yourself by trying on the gowns that hang in the closet over there. If they need alteration, I will send in our seamstress." She left me then, locking the door behind her.

I had no idea what kind of work I was supposed to do until the maid, a rather sweet Irish girl, brought my dinner.

When I asked her if she knew what would be required of me, she looked distressed. "Don't you *know*, Miss Angélique?" she asked.

"My name is Angela," I said. "You must have me confused with someone else."

"Oh no, Miss," she said. "The Madame said you was to be called Miss Angélique. French, you know."

"And what will she expect me to do?"

"Oh, miss, I hate to be the one to tell you! She'll want you to entertain the gentlemen who come here."

Oct. 31. What a shock that was, Maudie! At first I thought the girl must be mistaken, but she wasn't. The next day, Mrs. Williams spelled it all out for me. I was indeed to be known as Miss Angélique, and was to wait in my room every evening, dressed in one of the gowns that hung in the closet, until summoned to the parlor. There she would introduce me to a gentleman, and if he fancied my looks ("you may be sure he will, my dear") he would ask if he might see where I lived. I was to acquiesce gracefully and lead the way up to my room where I would make myself "agreeable" to him.

"Your esteemed husband used to patronize this house when my sister was alive," she said. "You didn't know that, did you? But he knew that I knew and paid me well to hold my tongue. And he will go on paying me because he knows I can ruin his reputation in a matter of minutes. Now maybe you understand why he wouldn't dismiss me when you asked him to—oh yes, I knew about that. But don't worry about him, my dear. I will not reveal your presence here. I am still in touch with him, you see.''

She said she knew he'd pay her well for turning me over to him, but first she wanted to give me a chance to work off my debt. She looked so cruel when she said that, Maudie. Then she smiled, an awful smile, and said that if I didn't behave, she'd make sure he came for me. I think what she really wanted to do was humiliate me, and she almost did.

Nov. 1. I was so shocked and terrified at the prospect of what lay before me that I couldn't say a word when she finished outlining my duties, and I suppose she decided I had given in. I hadn't, though. I spent every waking moment trying to think of a way to escape, and finally I hit on a plan that I thought would work. When I was summoned to the parlor two nights later, I was determined to *make* it work. I was also frightened half to death.

My heart sank when I saw the stocky middle-aged man standing in front of the fireplace, a most unattractive specimen in spite of the expensive evening clothes he was wearing. I was dressed in a particularly seductive low-cut silvery satin gown that clung to my figure, and I saw Mrs. Williams nod approvingly as she murmured that this was a Mr. Busby, from Dallas.

The man's eyes bulged as he extended both hands and moved across the room toward me.

''My sakes alive, sugar,'' he exclaimed, ''you're some dish, worth every penny. Show me where you live, huh?''

I had purposely left my room in a chaotic state—the bed unmade, clothes strewn about, and used towels thrown on the floor, a real mess—so that I could suggest that we'd be more comfortable in his hotel room. I was certain I could elude him before we got there. As luck would have it, there was no necessity for that ploy (it occurred to me later that I might not have been able to get past Robert). I nodded pleasantly to Mr. Busby, and he smiled eagerly at me. As he took my arm, I could smell liquor on his breath, and I thought he stumbled slightly as we headed for the stairs. Disgusting.

Just at that moment there was a great rattling of locks and bolts being undone as Robert admitted another "caller." The newcomer, a big man, pushed the door wide open, and I just had time to see his lewd glance at me before I broke away from Mr. Busby and ran out through the open door into the night.

I never looked back.

Nov. 2. Gregory was almost frantic with worry by the time I appeared in that ridiculous gown and absolutely furious when he heard what had happened to me. He was all for going to the police, but Henry Cope dissuaded him. It wouldn't do any good, Henry said, because such a house almost certainly paid protection money and we'd never get satisfaction. We had to do something, though. You see, I was afraid to go outdoors since Mrs. Williams knew I must be in the neighborhood. We were, after all, only a block and a half away from her, and she'd undoubtedly be on the lookout for me or even send Robert on a search.

Things went from bad to worse. There was no money coming in, and we had almost none left. I tried to phone you on Thanksgiving Day, and when no one answered, Gregory said he'd go up to Thirty-second Street and see if there was any money in the shoe box. I gave him my key, and he got in all right, but when he heard someone cough, he slipped out again. It was his idea, Maudie, not mine, but I did nothing to stop him. I should have.

In the end we moved to a cheap rooming house over near

Third Avenue, but we couldn't stay there long. Earlier in the fall Gregory had caught cold while painting a sign on a building, and he coughed so much at night that the other tenants complained. We were asked to leave.

From then on, we had a terrible time. We tried other rooming houses, cheap ones, and when our money was almost gone, we had to settle for the most wretched place I've ever seen—a dreadful filthy room in a tenement on Greenwich Street. I won't even tell you what it looked like, but it was no place for a sick man, and Gregory's cough was worse than ever.

We didn't even have our clothes with us. The landlady in the last place we'd lived in had kept them because we were so far behind in the rent. Gregory had offered to paint her picture for her in part payment, but she wouldn't hear of it. And she even kept his paints and brushes.

I knew we couldn't stay in that filthy place, Maudie, and we hadn't been there more than a couple of hours when I decided I had to ask you for help. I hated begging, but what else could I do? Gregory needed medicine so badly and a clean bed to sleep in.

So I wrote you a note and went outside to find a boy to deliver it. After that, I walked up the street a little way to see if I could find a store where I could buy some bread and cheese. I hadn't gone very far when I heard footsteps behind me and a moment later I felt a hand on my arm.

And then that awful man Robert was telling me that Mrs. Williams wanted to see me.

"She sent me to find you," he said. "I bin lookin' for days. Now maybe she'll let up on me."

He let go of my arm, and when he didn't threaten to drag me off, I smiled at him, thanked him for giving me the message, and told him to tell her I'd be along later on. He nodded—he was a stupid oaf—and stood aside to let me pass.

When I got back to the tenement (I never did buy the bread and cheese), I saw him on the other side of the street watching me. I waved to him, and he waved back. Then he went away, and I went inside to wait for you.

But I couldn't wait, not after what happened.

It seemed like hours and hours before I heard someone at the door. I thought it was you, Maudie, and when I saw Derek standing there, I nearly fainted. I tried to shut the door on him, but I couldn't, and all at once he had his arm around me and was saying something about taking me home with him—I remember thinking that Robert must have told Mrs. Williams where I was and that she'd phoned him.

Anyway, there he was, trying to kiss me! Gregory had been sitting at the table in the middle of the room with his head in his hands, and when he saw Derek take hold of me, he jumped up and pulled him away. They had an awful fight, Maudie— terrible! Gregory was bigger than Derek, and even though he was sick, he seemed to be getting the better of him until Derek picked up a knife that was on the table. I saw Gregory try to grab his wrist, but he couldn't and Derek slashed at him, forcing him to back across the room until he collapsed on a cot against the wall. Derek was on him in a second, and I saw blood all over. Then there was a frightening gurgling sound— that's when I ran out of the place.

(Angie had been clutching my hand so hard through the telling of this episode that I was afraid she'd be worn out, so I told her I had to leave but would be back tomorrow. When I arrived the next afternoon, the nurse said Angie had been asking for me, and almost before I was seated next to the bed, she went on with her story.)

Nov. 3. I don't know what I was thinking of, Maudie, leaving Gregory like that. We'd loved each other, really *loved* each other, and I should at least have seen that he had a decent burial, but I was too intent on getting away from Derek. I started for Thirty-second Street, running as fast as I could so he wouldn't catch up with me, but I was all mixed up, half crazy, I guess, because I suddenly found myself down in Little Germany—you know, where we lived once.

I can't imagine why I went there, but it was probably fortunate that I ran downtown instead of uptown because I'd never told Derek anything about our early life. I just let him believe we'd always lived on Thirty-second Street, so I didn't think it would occur to him to look for me on Eleventh Street.

It hadn't changed very much, and when I recognized Carlotta Schwartz's house, I knocked on the door. We always liked Carlotta, remember? She'd never married. She just stayed home and took care of her mother and father, since both of them suffered from rheumatism. Such good, kind people! They took me in without a word and asked no questions. Mrs. Schwartz (I think she was becoming a little senile) kept calling me her "poor motherless child" and talked about the *Slocum* tragedy until Mr. Schwartz made her stop.

It took me a long time, several months, I think, to get over Gregory's death. No, that's not right, Maudie—I've never gotten over it completely. At first I didn't want to go out. I just wanted to hide, but I knew I couldn't do that forever. I think it was sometime in March of that year that I first went outdoors, and early in April Carlotta helped me find a job in a shirt factory on Houston Street. Mr. Schwartz had worked there for years and put in a good word for me.

The hours were long, but I didn't mind the work, and my wages enabled me to pay the Schwartzes a little for my board. I was able to buy some clothes too, which I needed badly, just essentials, nothing fancy, but I always made sure I looked attractive during working hours. You see, they'd put me at the showcase where the buyers came to look for the latest styles in shirts.

That's where I met Edgar. He's the owner of a posh men's clothing store in London and came in to order for the fall season. You'll like him when you meet him, Maudie. I've been very happy with him. He's gentle and kind, and ever so good-looking. Well, that's how I met him—in the shirt factory.

Once in a while I was afraid that Mrs. Williams or Derek would come looking for me, but they never did, and eventually I stopped jumping every time the doorbell rang. I'll never forgive him, Maudie—Derek, I mean. He ruined my life twice. First by marrying me, and then by killing my lover. If Gregory had lived, we would have been all right. He really had talent, and if you'd helped us—I know you would have—he would have recovered his health and made enough money to pay for a trip abroad. He wanted to go to France. Of course, I did go abroad later, as you know, with Edgar, but that was after I did what I knew I had to do.

Edgar wanted to marry me right away, but I couldn't until . . . oh, I'll tell you tomorrow.

Nov. 4. All the time I was working in the shirt factory I was making plans, and when I'd saved up a few dollars, I was ready to act. I left the Schwartz household, telling them I'd found a better position uptown and wanted to live nearer to where I'd be working. They didn't want me to leave.

On my last night with them I took an ice pick from the kitchen. I didn't want to buy one, for fear a salesgirl would remember selling it to me, so I just slipped it into the pocket of my skirt after the evening meal when I was helping Carlotta with the dishes. Then, the next day—I remember it was Friday, the twenty-seventh of August; I'll never forget that date as long as I live—I took the train to Tarrytown. I wore a plain black dress and black gloves (I remembered how Mama used to say that a lady always wore dark clothes when traveling) and kept my eyes lowered during the trip. Once in Tarrytown, I left the village and went by back roads and paths through the woods—a couple of miles, I guess—to Blauvelt House. By the middle of the afternoon I was at the edge of the estate. It was an awfully hot day, and no one was in the gardens or on the lawns. I knew they all rested and took it easy on afternoons like that one, and I was counting on Derek's taking his usual nap in the study.

I stood behind some shrubbery until I was sure the coast was clear, then tiptoed across the terrace. One of the French doors was open, and I slipped inside without making any noise. Derek was there, asleep on the couch, with his mouth open—disgusting.

(While Angie paused, I held my breath, terrified of what I might hear.)

He never made a sound, Maudie. I stabbed him in the throat with the ice pick and then stabbed him again to make sure he was dead. Blood spurted out, but none got on me, thank God. After that, I left the way I had come, satisfied that I was even with him at last. Then, when I stood for a moment behind some bushes and looked out over the gardens, so quiet and peaceful in the August sun, I was suddenly frightened. I think I expected to be struck down or dragged off in chains, but nothing happened, and after a few minutes I stopped shaking and went on.

You see, when Papa died, I felt nothing—no fear, no remorse, nothing at all—and I'd expected killing Derek would be the same, but it wasn't. For years I was afraid I'd be found out. You can see now why I stayed away and never gave you my address.

I can't imagine why the police blamed Derek's death on Mrs. Williams. She was an evil woman, but she was nobody's fool and knew that she'd get money out of Derek only if he remained alive. I wonder if she'd have been convicted if she hadn't gone insane.

I have no recollection of the train trip back to the city that day, but I remember walking over to the East River and throwing my gloves and the ice pick into the water. I even put some stones in the gloves so they'd sink. Then I went straight to Edgar's rooms at the Buckingham Hotel. The only thing that worried me was that I couldn't find my handkerchief. It was the last monogrammed one I had too.

We left New York the next day. Edgar had to make a tour of western cities, and I was more than willing to go with him. We were married in Chicago and went on from there to San Francisco. I forget where else we went. I was just glad to be out of New York. We didn't come back here until just before Christmas—I phoned you, remember? And that was only for one night. It worried me to be in the city, but I'm not worried any longer. It's all so far away now, and I'm so tired. I just hope Edgar comes in time. . . .

(Angie's voice failed then, and she looked so exhausted that I thought she'd drift off to sleep. A moment later, though, she seized my hand and clung to it while a sudden spasm of pain racked her body. I rang frantically for the nurse, who administered a sedative. When Angie's grip on my hand relaxed, I slipped away and walked blindly home, my mind in turmoil.)

Nov. 5. (When I returned to the hospital today, I was told that Angie was in a coma and sinking rapidly. Edgar arrived while I was sitting at her bedside. Together we watched until the end came.)

Epilogue

A few weeks after Angie's funeral Tom advised me to burn my notes. "Edgar's a fine fellow, honey," he said, "and I wouldn't want him to see them, ever. There's no reason to destroy his image of Angie. And think of the effect such revelations would have on Kitty and Megan if they came across them! It's enough that you and I know the truth."

I couldn't bring myself to burn them then. Shocking as they were, they seemed to be all I had left of my sister. I kept them locked in a drawer in my desk for more than five years, taking them out occasionally when something reminded me of her. I brought them with me when I came down here to Florida, and now I have reread them for the last time.

The doctors say I have completely regained my health, and Tom is coming the day after tomorrow to take me home. It would not be possible to burn the notes here since the only fireplace is in the main parlor downstairs, but when I am back in my own house, I shall consign them, page by page, to the fire in my sitting room when I am alone. Once they are gone, I hope I'll be able to remember Angie as she was before another fire changed our lives irrevocably, not as she was afterward.

FEB 2 4 1992

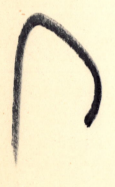